the Archie® DIGEST LIBRARY

Jughead® with Archie®

– in –

Wish Fulfillment

Spotlight

visit us at
www.abdopublishing.com

Exclusive Spotlight library bound edition published in 2007 by Spotlight, a division of ABDO Publishing Group, Edina, Minnesota. Spotlight produces high quality reinforced library bound editions for schools and libraries. Published by agreement with Archie Comic Publications, Inc.

Library of Congress Cataloging-in-Publication Data

Jughead with Archie in Wish fulfillment / edited by Nelson Ribeiro & Victor Gorelick.
   p. cm. -- (The Archie digest library)
   Revision of issue no. 195 (Oct. 2004) of Jughead with Archie digest magazine.
   ISBN-13: 978-1-59961-277-5
   ISBN-10: 1-59961-277-1
   1. Comic books, strips, etc. I. Ribeiro, Nelson. II. Gorelick, Victor. III. Jughead with Archie digest magazine. 195. IV. Title: Wish fulfillment.

PN6728.A72J89 2007
741.5'973--dc22

                        2006050691

All Spotlight books are reinforced library binding
and manufactured in the United States of America.

Contents

Jughead® with Archie®

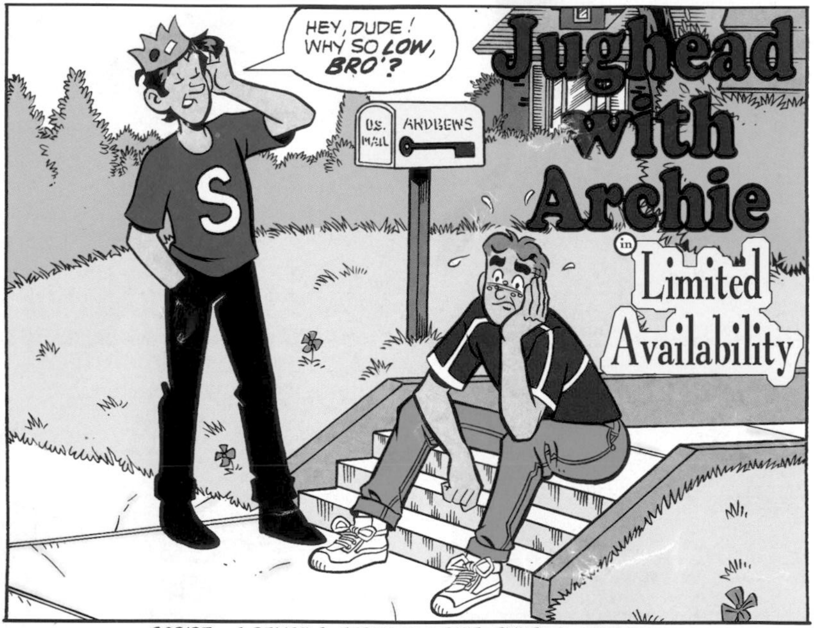

HEY, DUDE! WHY SO LOW, BRO'?
U.S. MAIL
ANDREWS
Jughead with Archie
in
Limited Availability

SCRIPT: & PENCILS: FERNANDO RUIZ INKS: AL MILGROM
COLORS: BARRY GROSSMAN LETTERS: BILL YOSHIDA
EDITORS: NELSON RIBEIRO & VICTOR GORELICK EDITOR-IN-CHIEF: RICHARD GOLDWATER

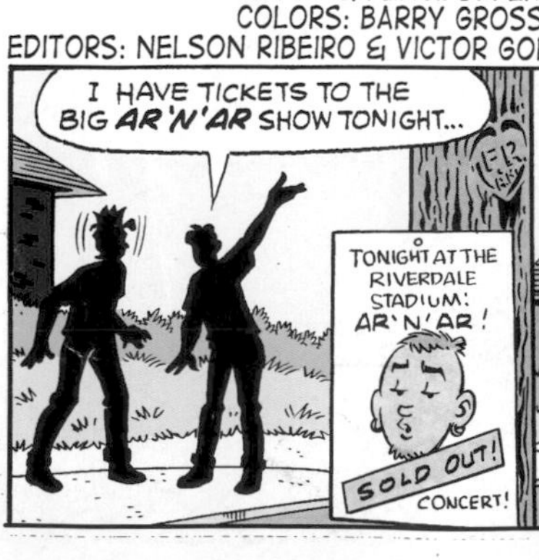

I HAVE TICKETS TO THE BIG AR'N'AR SHOW TONIGHT...
TONIGHT AT THE RIVERDALE STADIUM: AR'N'AR! CONCERT!
SOLD OUT!

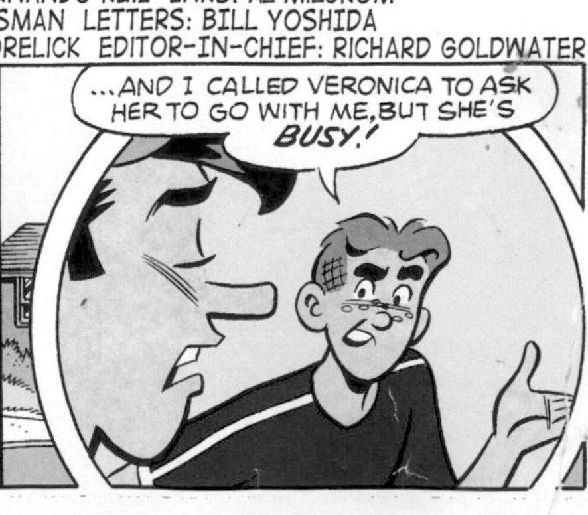

...AND I CALLED VERONICA TO ASK HER TO GO WITH ME, BUT SHE'S BUSY!

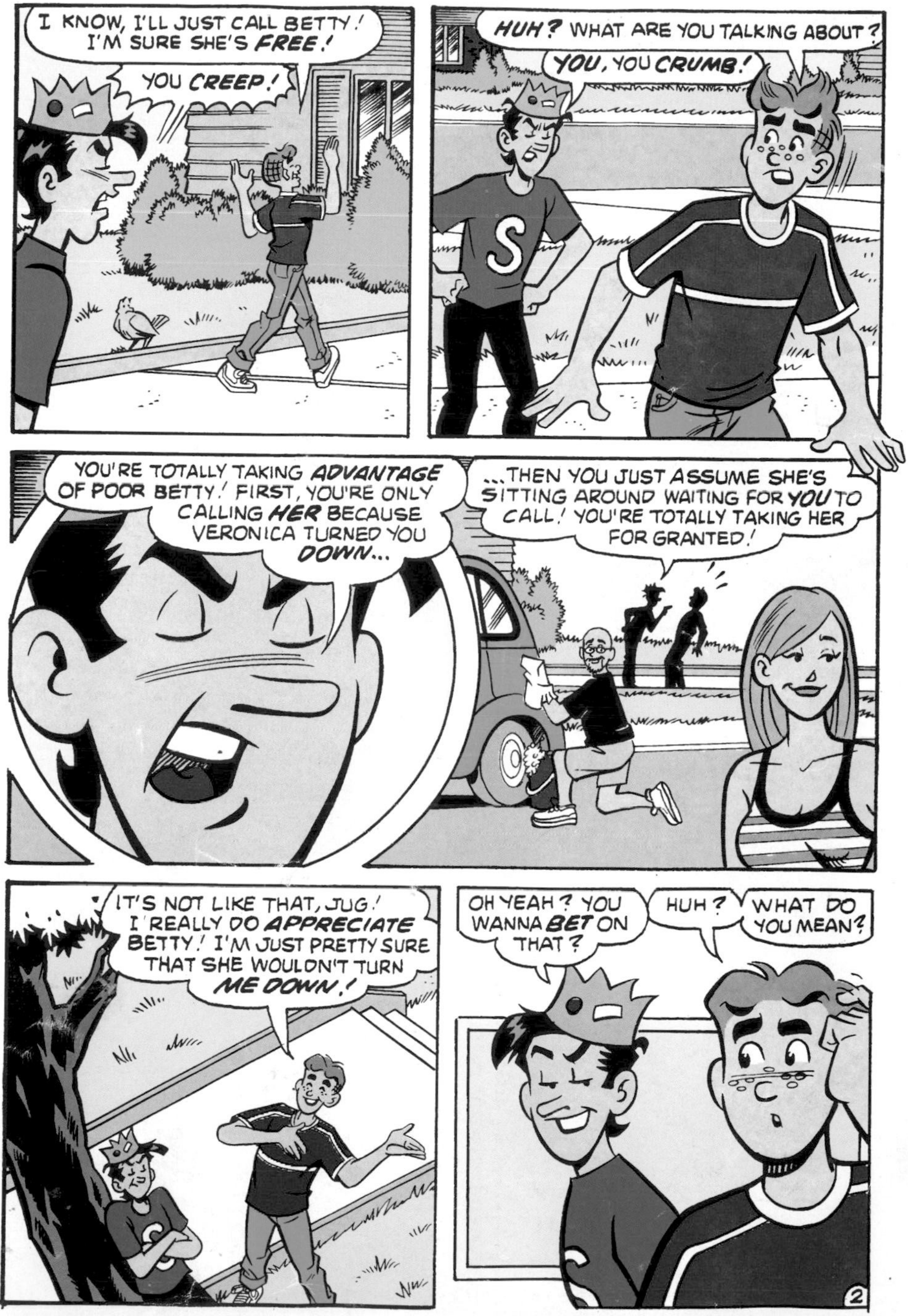
I KNOW, I'LL JUST CALL BETTY! I'M SURE SHE'S FREE!
YOU CREEP!
HUH? WHAT ARE YOU TALKING ABOUT?
YOU, YOU CRUMB!
YOU'RE TOTALLY TAKING ADVANTAGE OF POOR BETTY! FIRST, YOU'RE ONLY CALLING HER BECAUSE VERONICA TURNED YOU DOWN...
...THEN YOU JUST ASSUME SHE'S SITTING AROUND WAITING FOR YOU TO CALL! YOU'RE TOTALLY TAKING HER FOR GRANTED!
IT'S NOT LIKE THAT, JUG! I REALLY DO APPRECIATE BETTY! I'M JUST PRETTY SURE THAT SHE WOULDN'T TURN ME DOWN!
OH YEAH? YOU WANNA BET ON THAT?
HUH?
WHAT DO YOU MEAN?
2

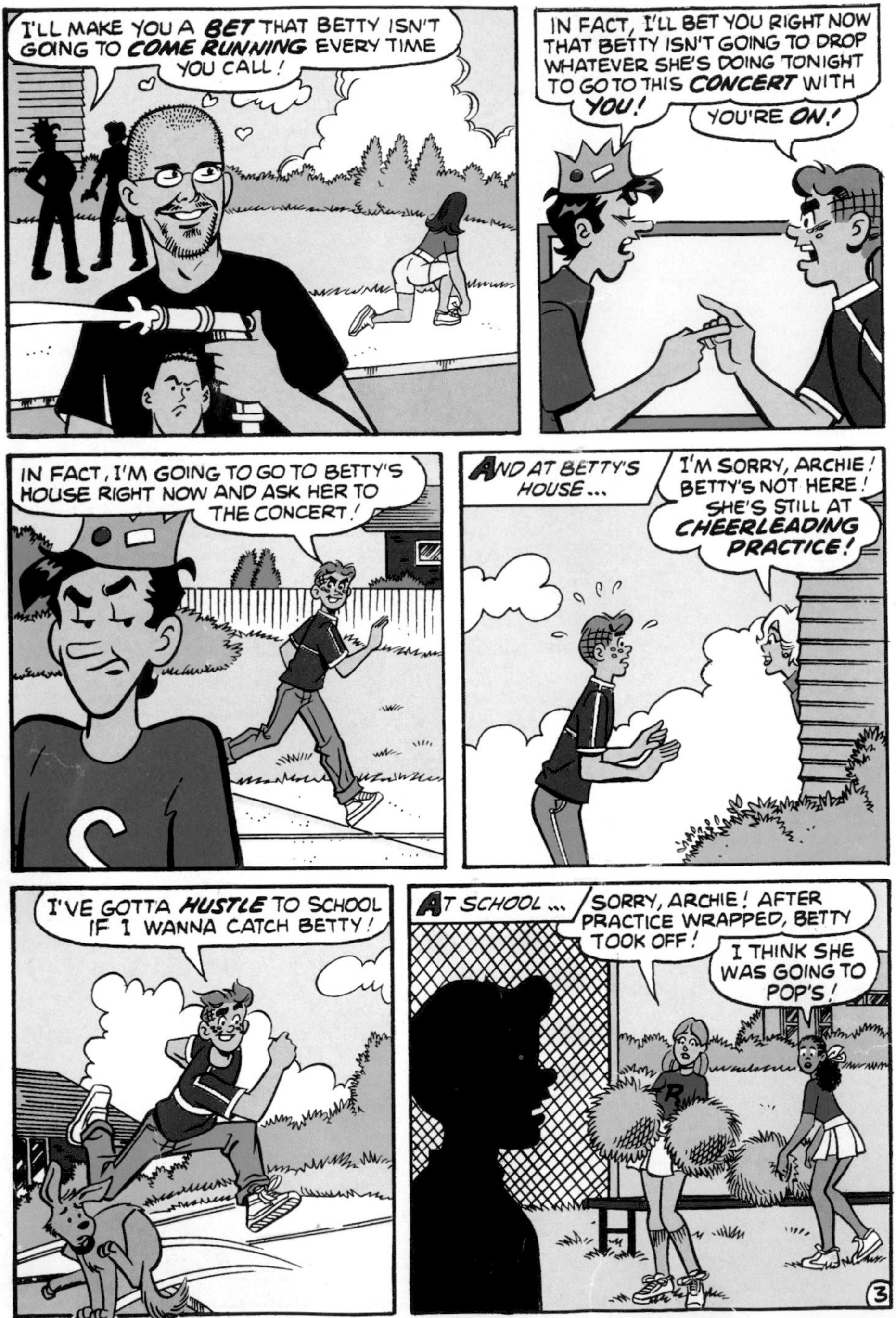
I'LL MAKE YOU A BET THAT BETTY ISN'T GOING TO COME RUNNING EVERY TIME YOU CALL!
IN FACT, I'LL BET YOU RIGHT NOW THAT BETTY ISN'T GOING TO DROP WHATEVER SHE'S DOING TONIGHT TO GO TO THIS CONCERT WITH YOU!
YOU'RE ON!
IN FACT, I'M GOING TO GO TO BETTY'S HOUSE RIGHT NOW AND ASK HER TO THE CONCERT!
AND AT BETTY'S HOUSE...
I'M SORRY, ARCHIE! BETTY'S NOT HERE! SHE'S STILL AT CHEERLEADING PRACTICE!
I'VE GOTTA HUSTLE TO SCHOOL IF I WANNA CATCH BETTY!
AT SCHOOL...
SORRY, ARCHIE! AFTER PRACTICE WRAPPED, BETTY TOOK OFF!
I THINK SHE WAS GOING TO POP'S!
3

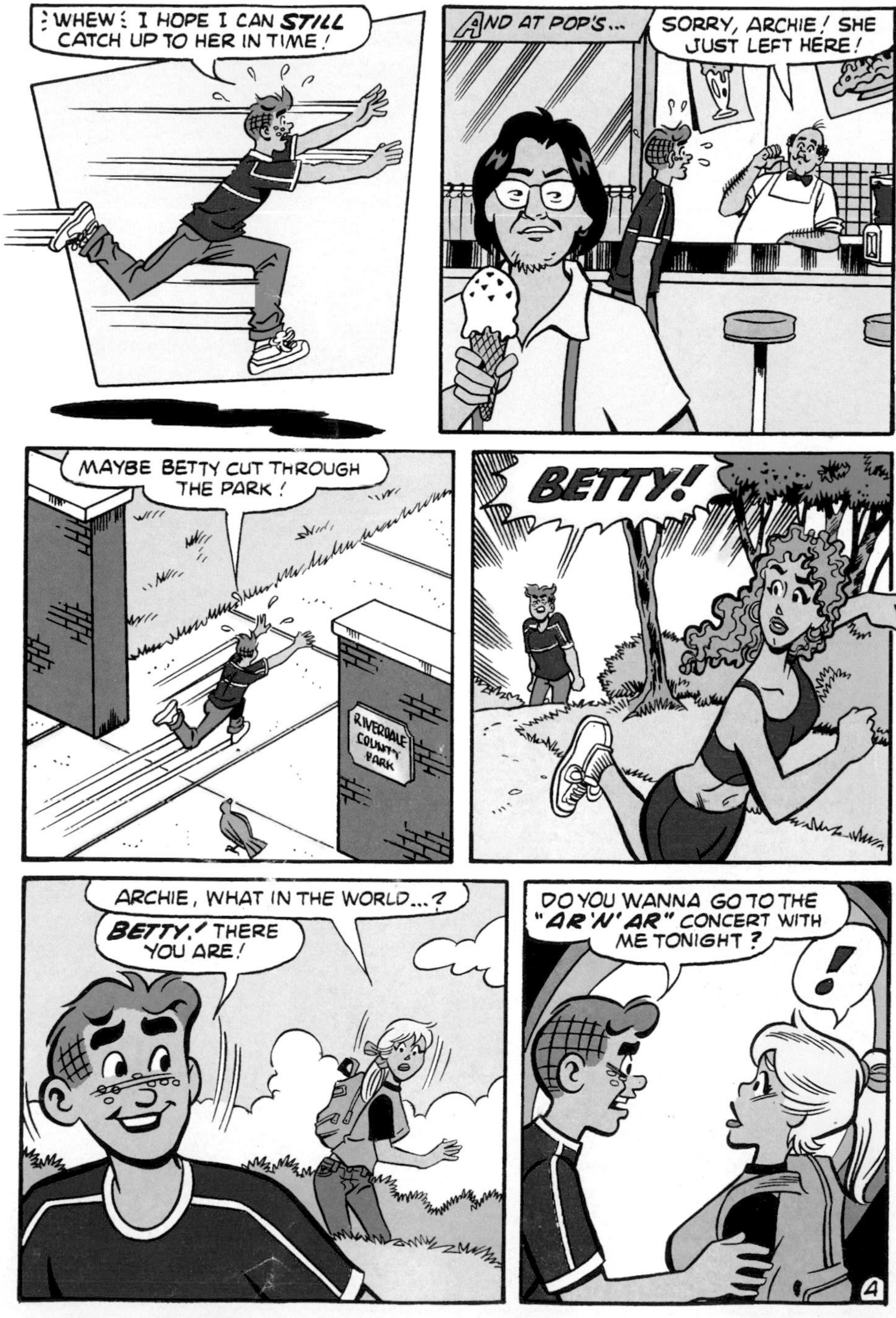
WHEW! I HOPE I CAN STILL CATCH UP TO HER IN TIME!
AND AT POP'S...
SORRY, ARCHIE! SHE JUST LEFT HERE!
MAYBE BETTY CUT THROUGH THE PARK!
RIVERDALE COUNTY PARK
BETTY!
ARCHIE, WHAT IN THE WORLD...?
BETTY! THERE YOU ARE!
DO YOU WANNA GO TO THE "AR'N'AR" CONCERT WITH ME TONIGHT?
!
4

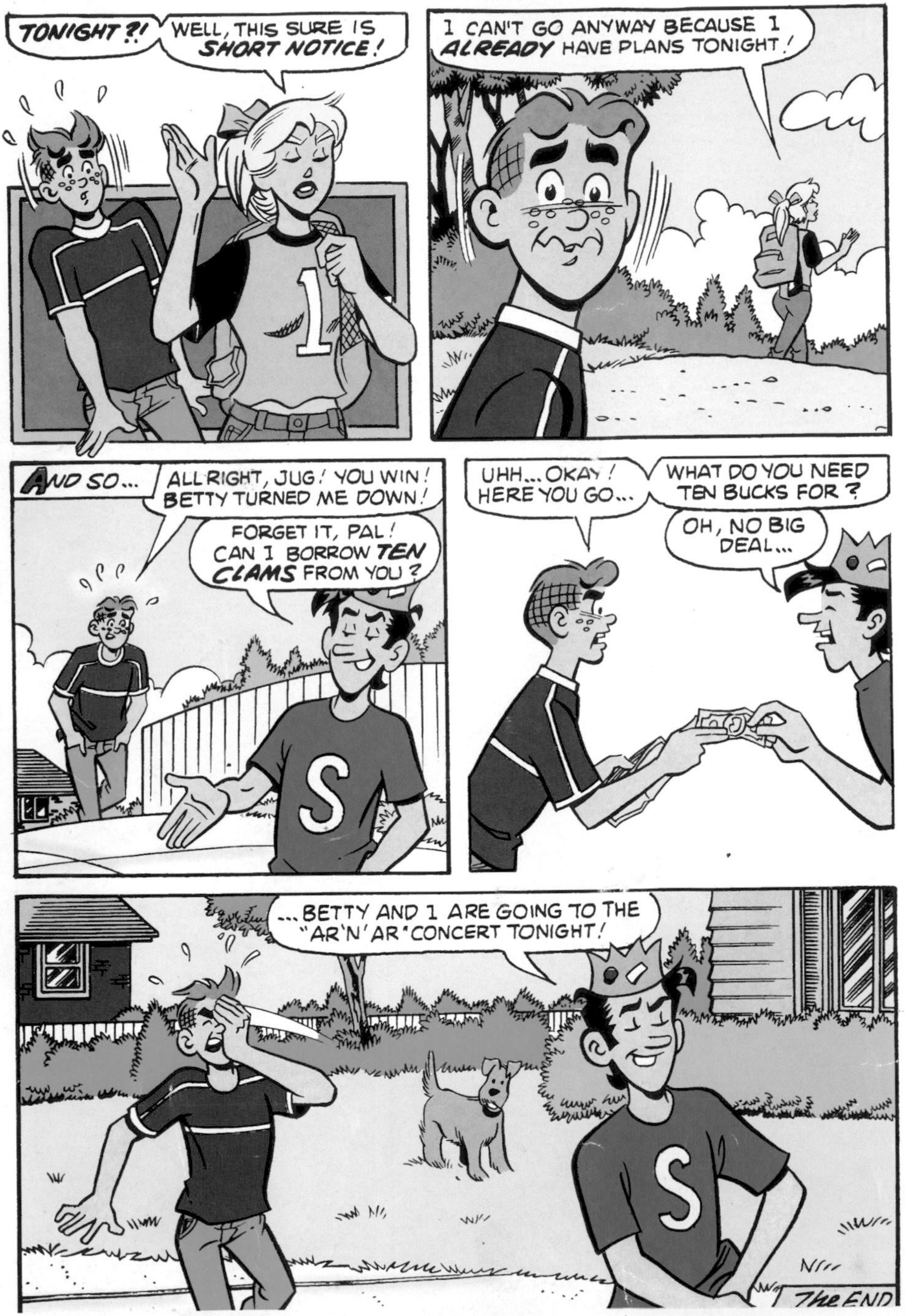
TONIGHT ?!
WELL, THIS SURE IS SHORT NOTICE!
I CAN'T GO ANYWAY BECAUSE I ALREADY HAVE PLANS TONIGHT!
AND SO...
ALL RIGHT, JUG! YOU WIN! BETTY TURNED ME DOWN!
FORGET IT, PAL! CAN I BORROW TEN CLAMS FROM YOU?
UHH... OKAY! HERE YOU GO...
WHAT DO YOU NEED TEN BUCKS FOR ?
OH, NO BIG DEAL...
...BETTY AND I ARE GOING TO THE "AR'N'AR" CONCERT TONIGHT!
The END

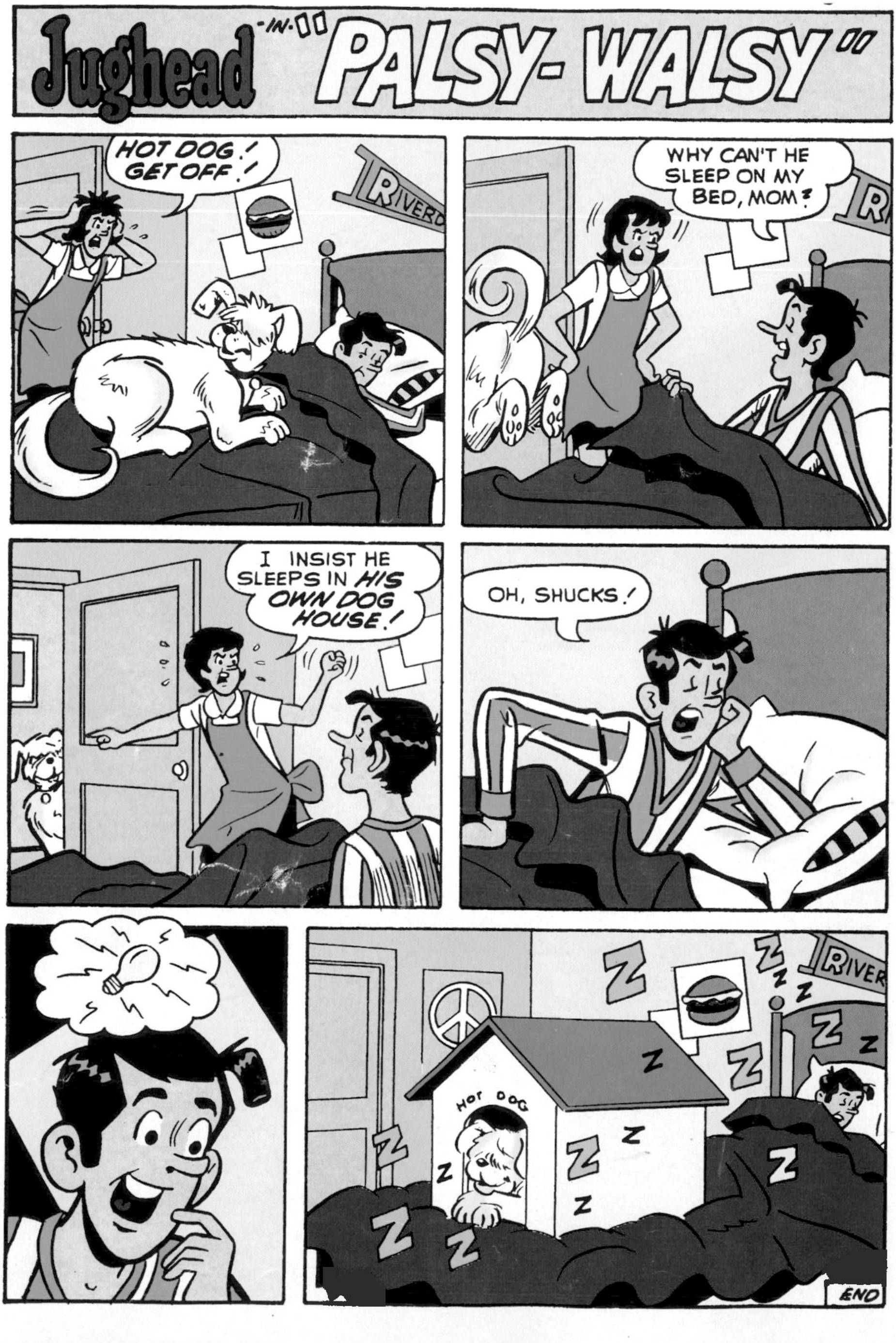
Jughead -IN- "PALSY-WALSY"
HOT DOG! GET OFF!
WHY CAN'T HE SLEEP ON MY BED, MOM?
I INSIST HE SLEEPS IN HIS OWN DOG HOUSE!
OH, SHUCKS!
HOT DOG
END

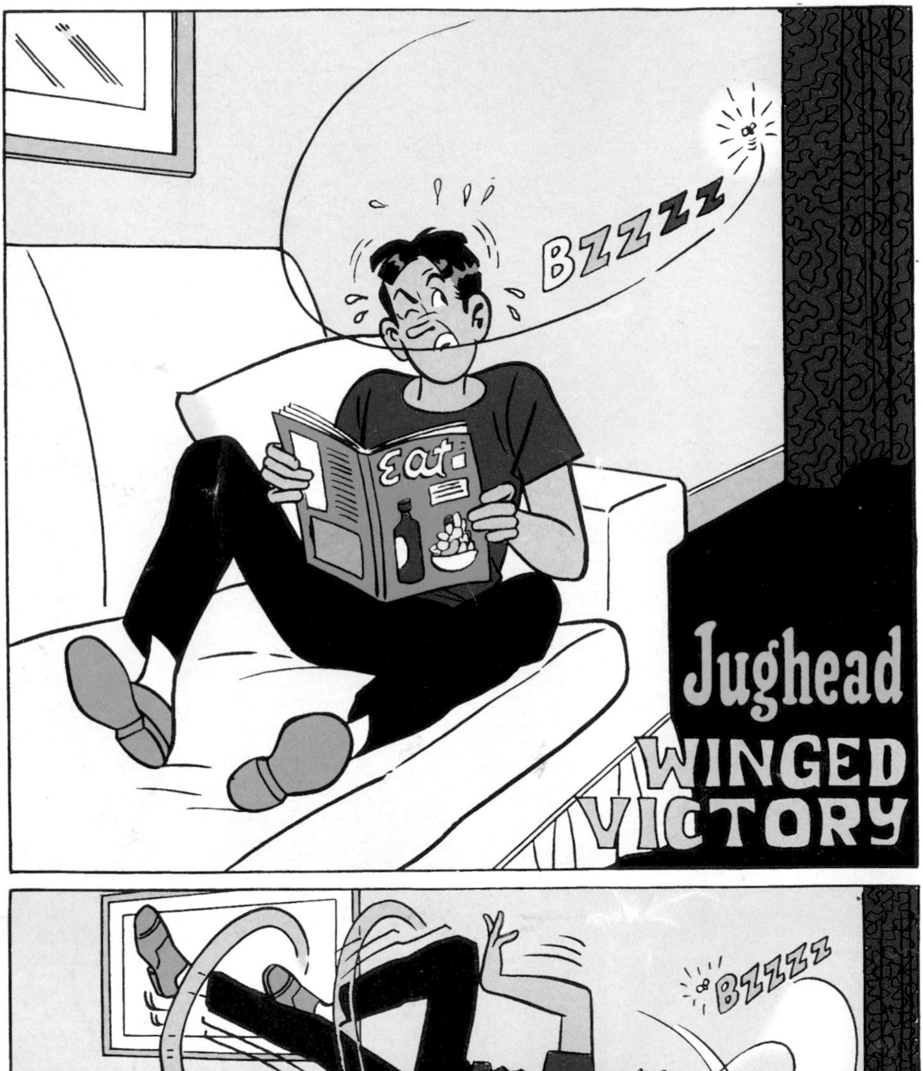
BZZZZ
Jughead
WINGED VICTORY
Eat

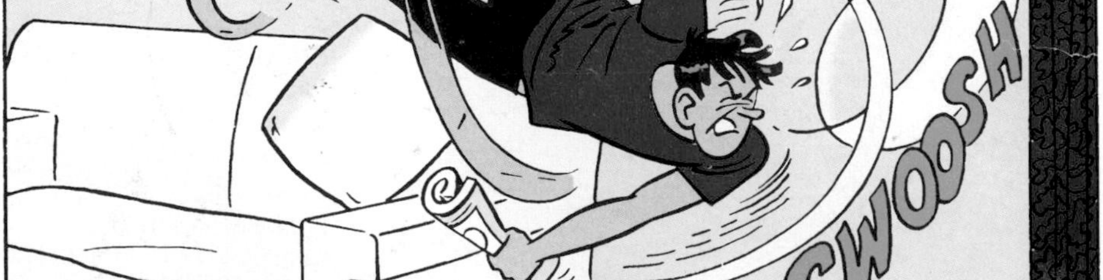
BZZZZ
SWOOSH

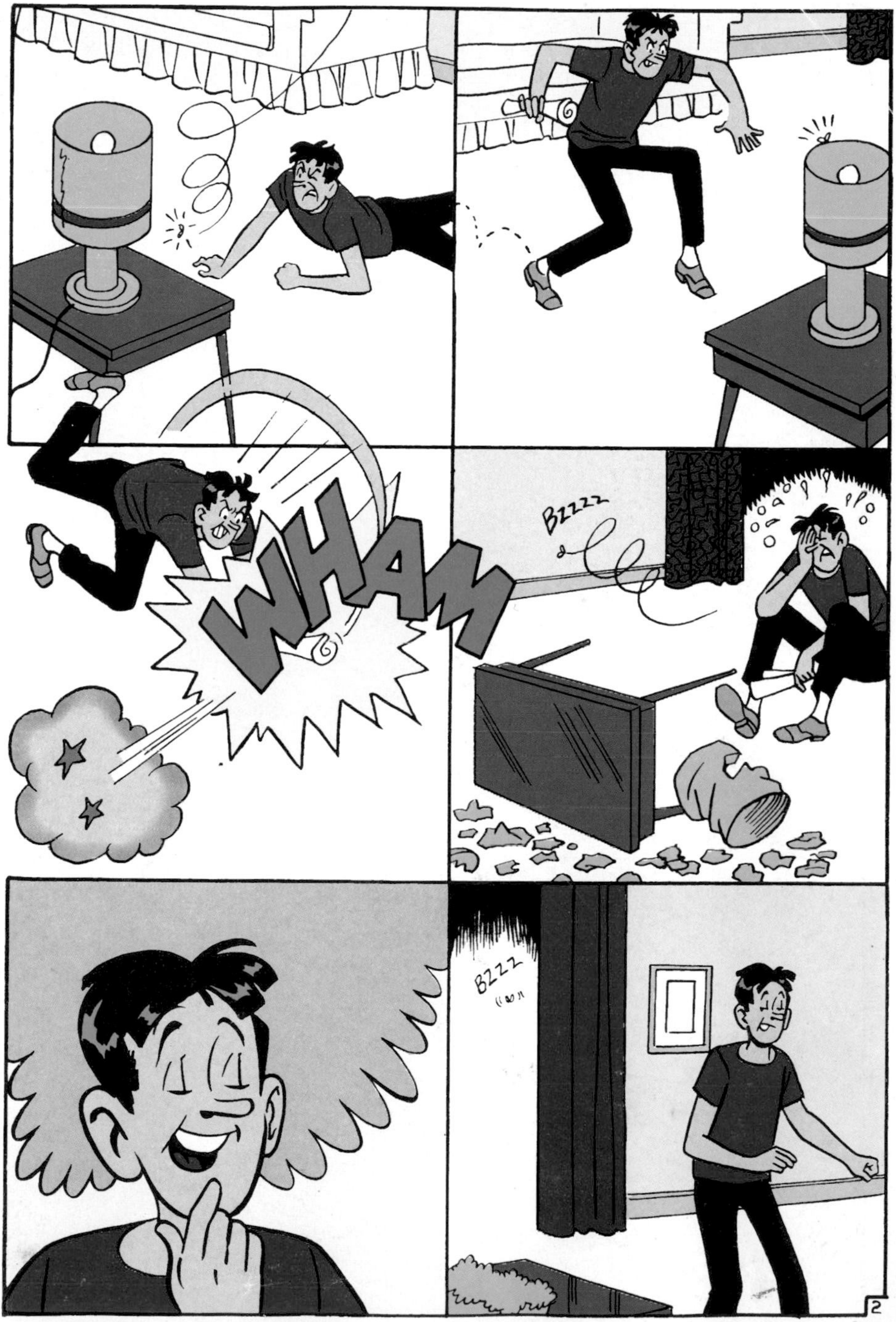
WHAM
BZZZZ
BZZZ

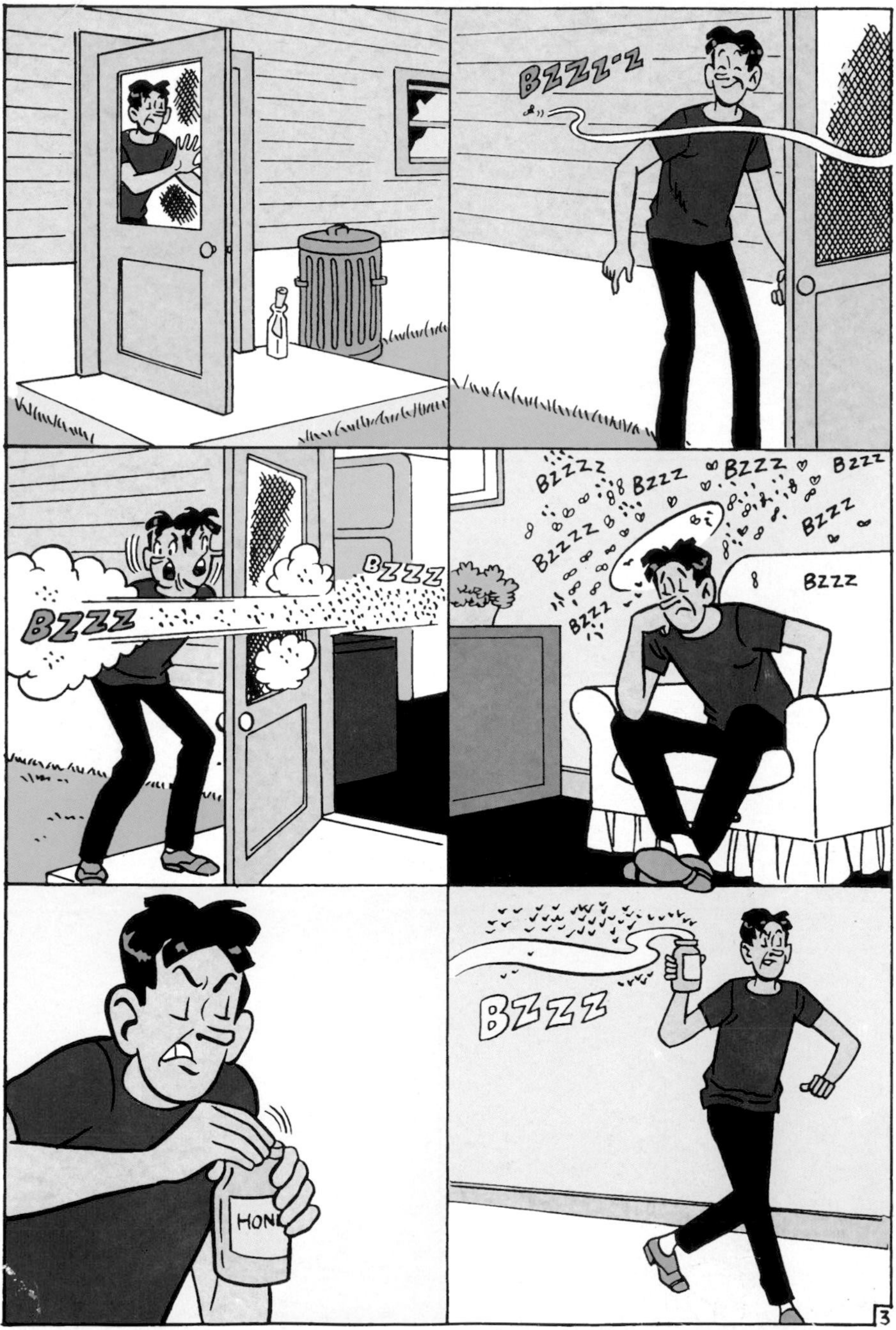
BZZZ-Z
BZZZ
BZZZ
BZZZZ
BZZZ
BZZZ
BZZZ
BZZZ
BZZZZ
BZZZ
BZZZ
BZZZ
HON
BZZZ
3

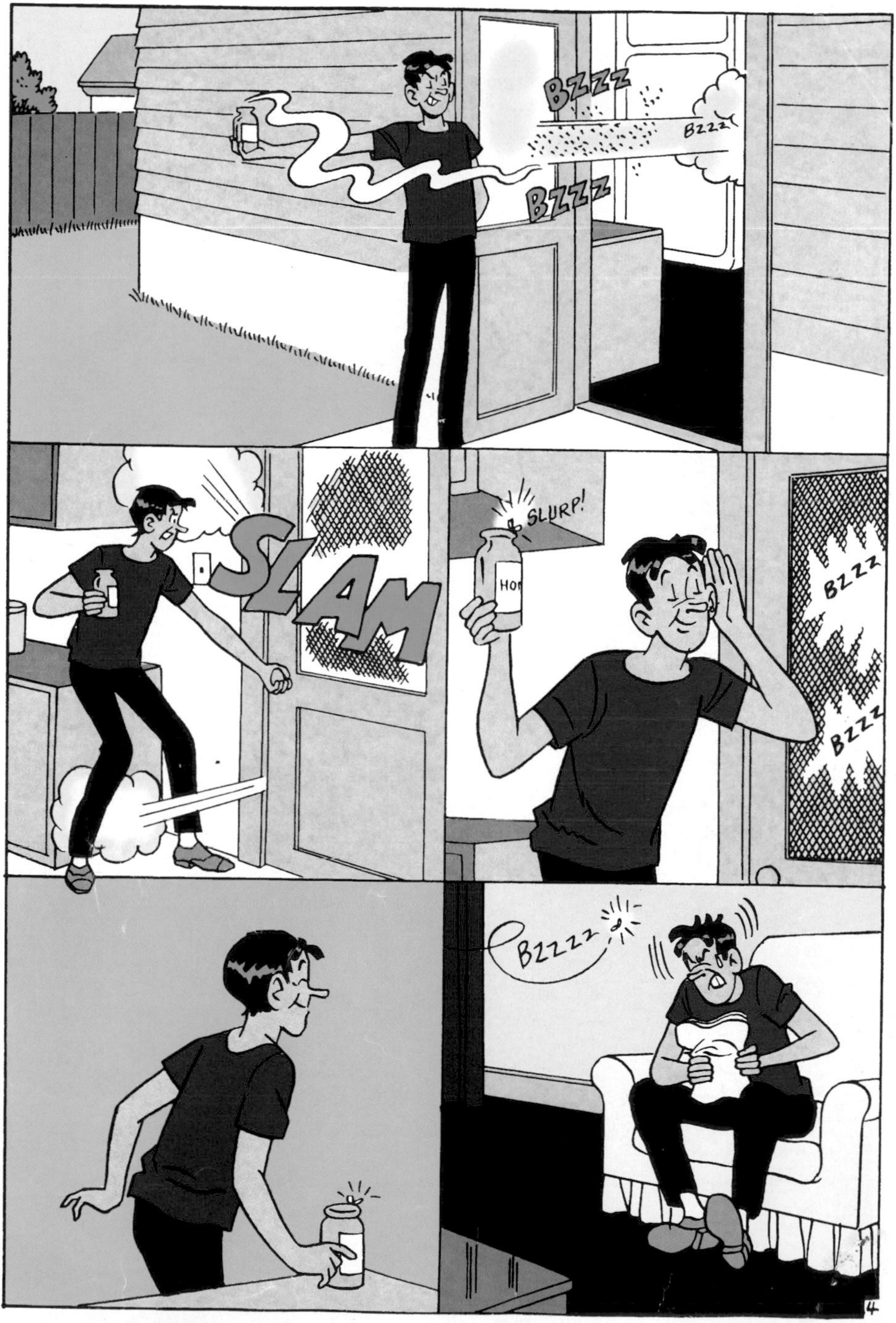
BZZZ
BZZZ
BZZZ
SLAM
SLURP!
HON
BZZZ
BZZZ
BZZZZ
4

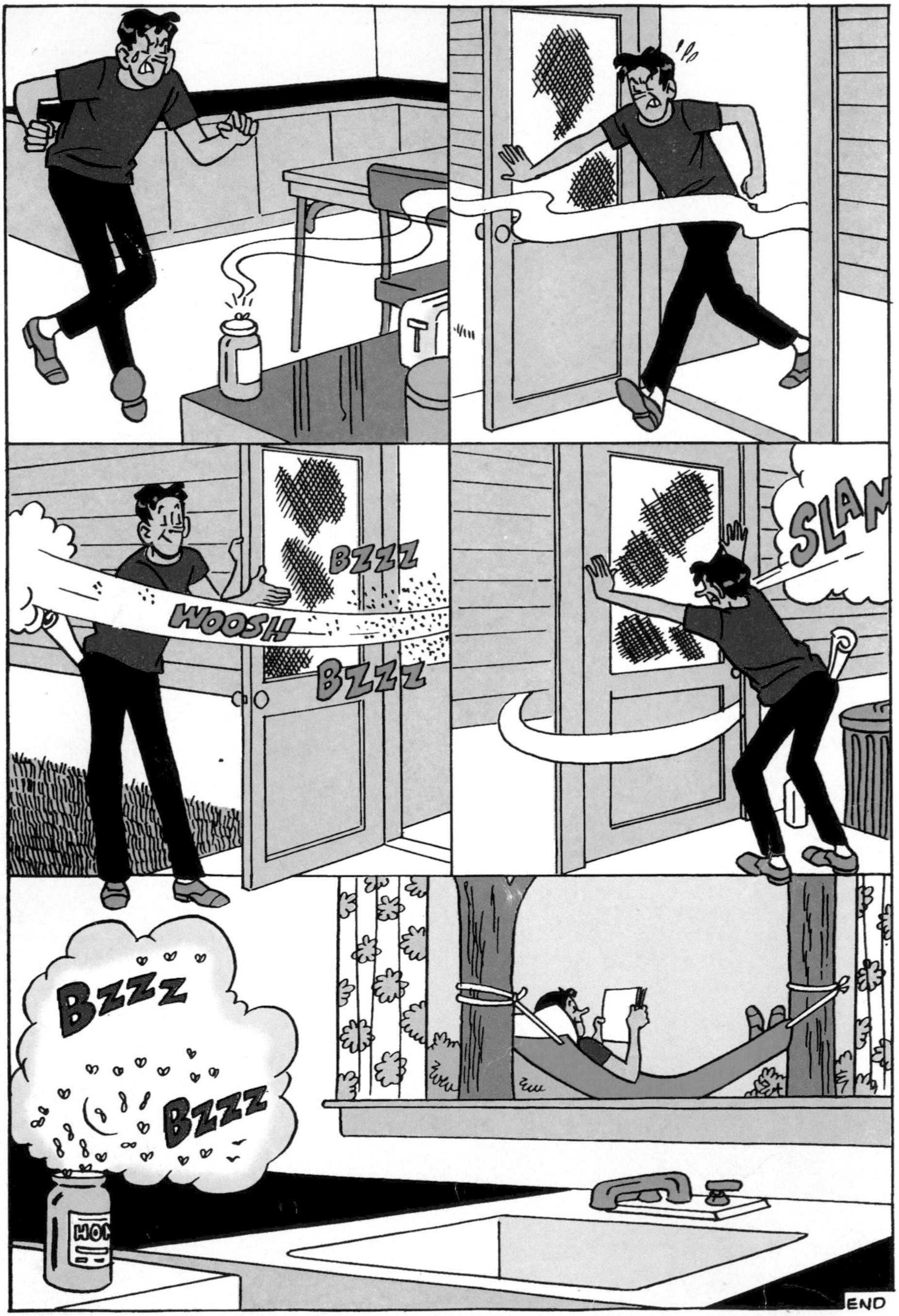
BZZZ
WOOSH
BZZZ
SLAM
Bzzz
Bzzz
END

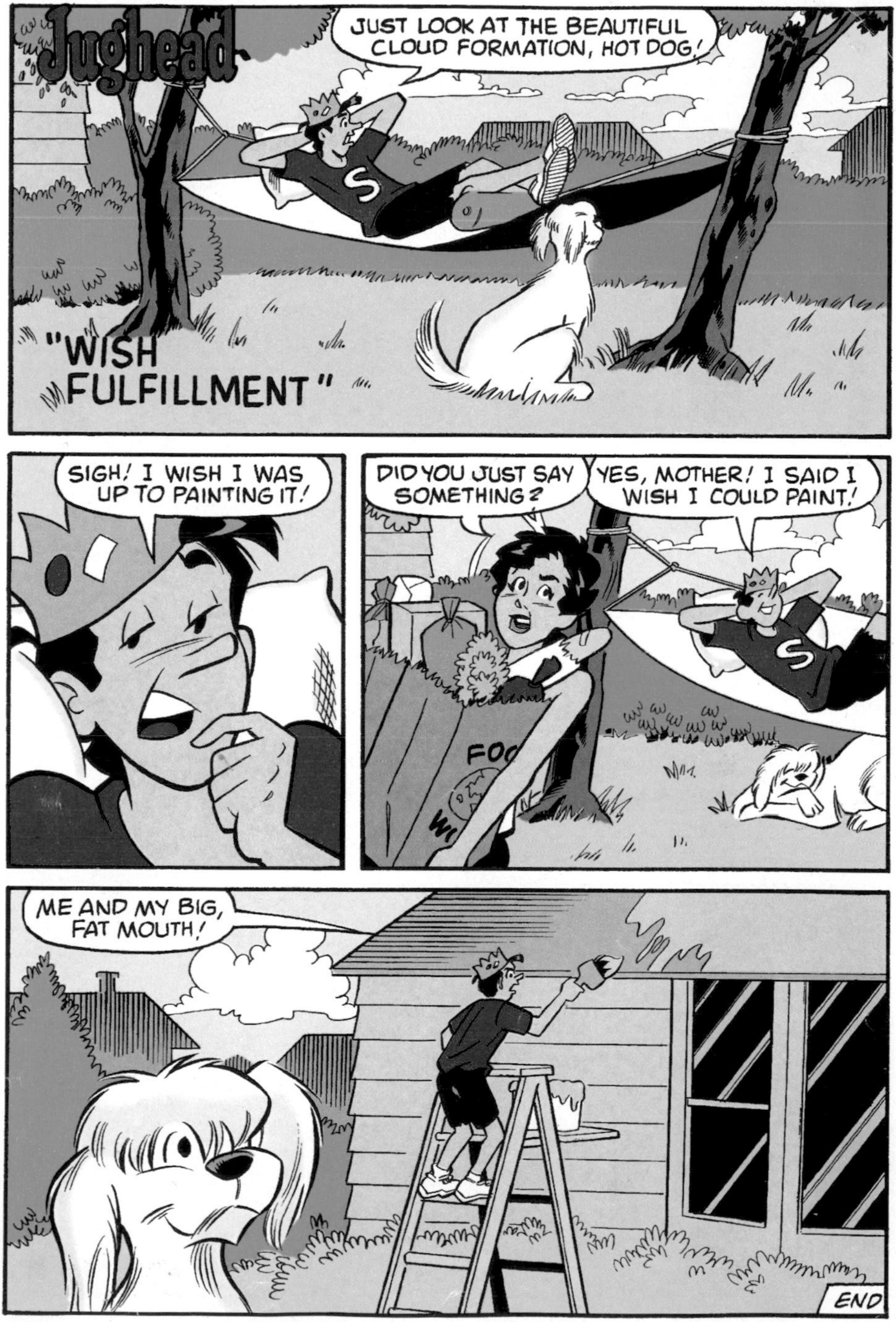
Jughead
JUST LOOK AT THE BEAUTIFUL CLOUD FORMATION, HOT DOG!
"WISH FULFILLMENT"
SIGH! I WISH I WAS UP TO PAINTING IT!
DID YOU JUST SAY SOMETHING?
YES, MOTHER! I SAID I WISH I COULD PAINT!
ME AND MY BIG, FAT MOUTH!
END

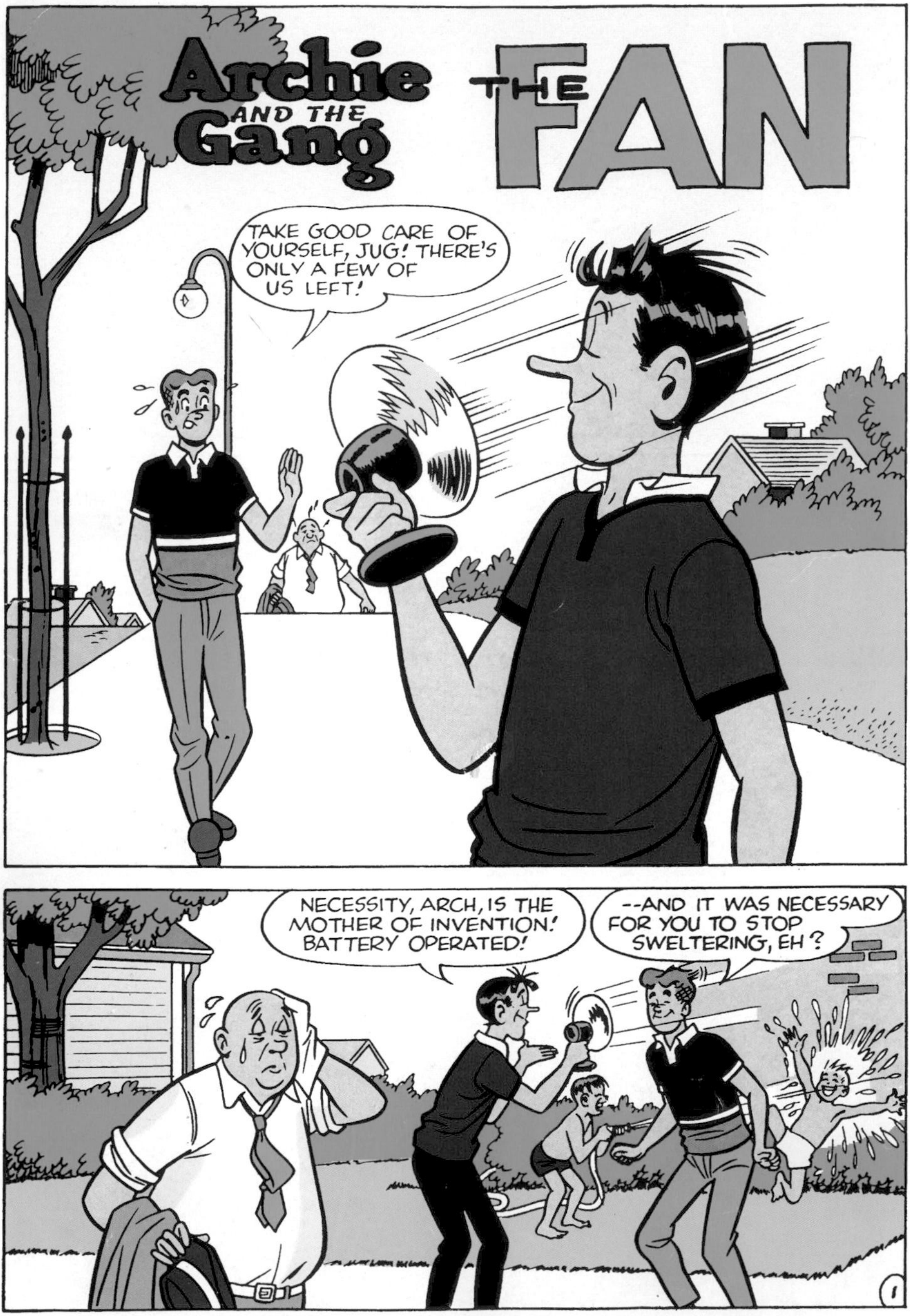
Archie AND THE Gang
THE FAN
TAKE GOOD CARE OF YOURSELF, JUG! THERE'S ONLY A FEW OF US LEFT!
NECESSITY, ARCH, IS THE MOTHER OF INVENTION! BATTERY OPERATED!
--AND IT WAS NECESSARY FOR YOU TO STOP SWELTERING, EH?
1

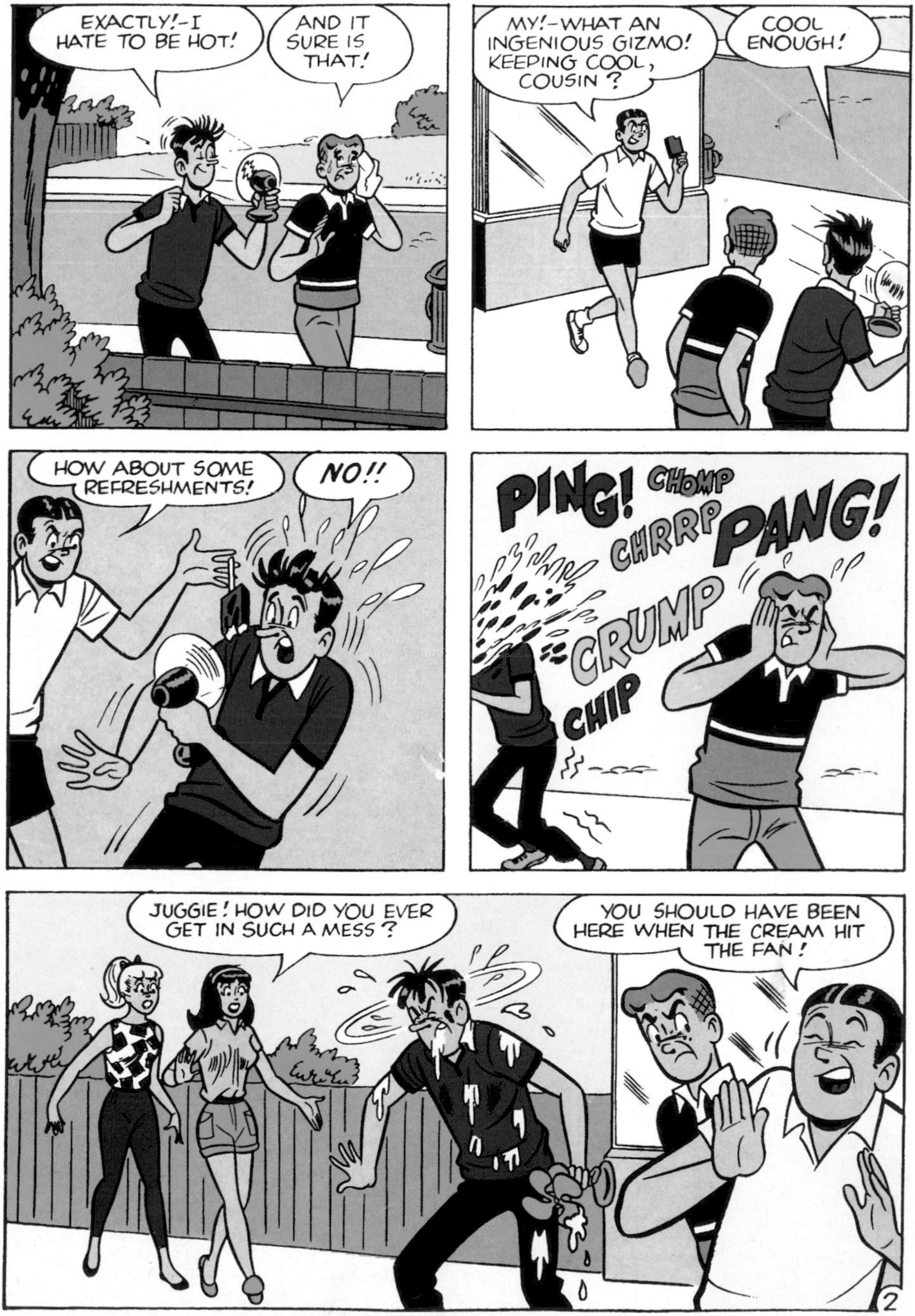
EXACTLY!-I HATE TO BE HOT!
AND IT SURE IS THAT!
MY!-WHAT AN INGENIOUS GIZMO! KEEPING COOL, COUSIN ?
COOL ENOUGH!
HOW ABOUT SOME REFRESHMENTS!
NO!!
PING! CHOMP
CHRRP PANG!
CRUMP
CHIP
JUGGIE! HOW DID YOU EVER GET IN SUCH A MESS ?
YOU SHOULD HAVE BEEN HERE WHEN THE CREAM HIT THE FAN!
2

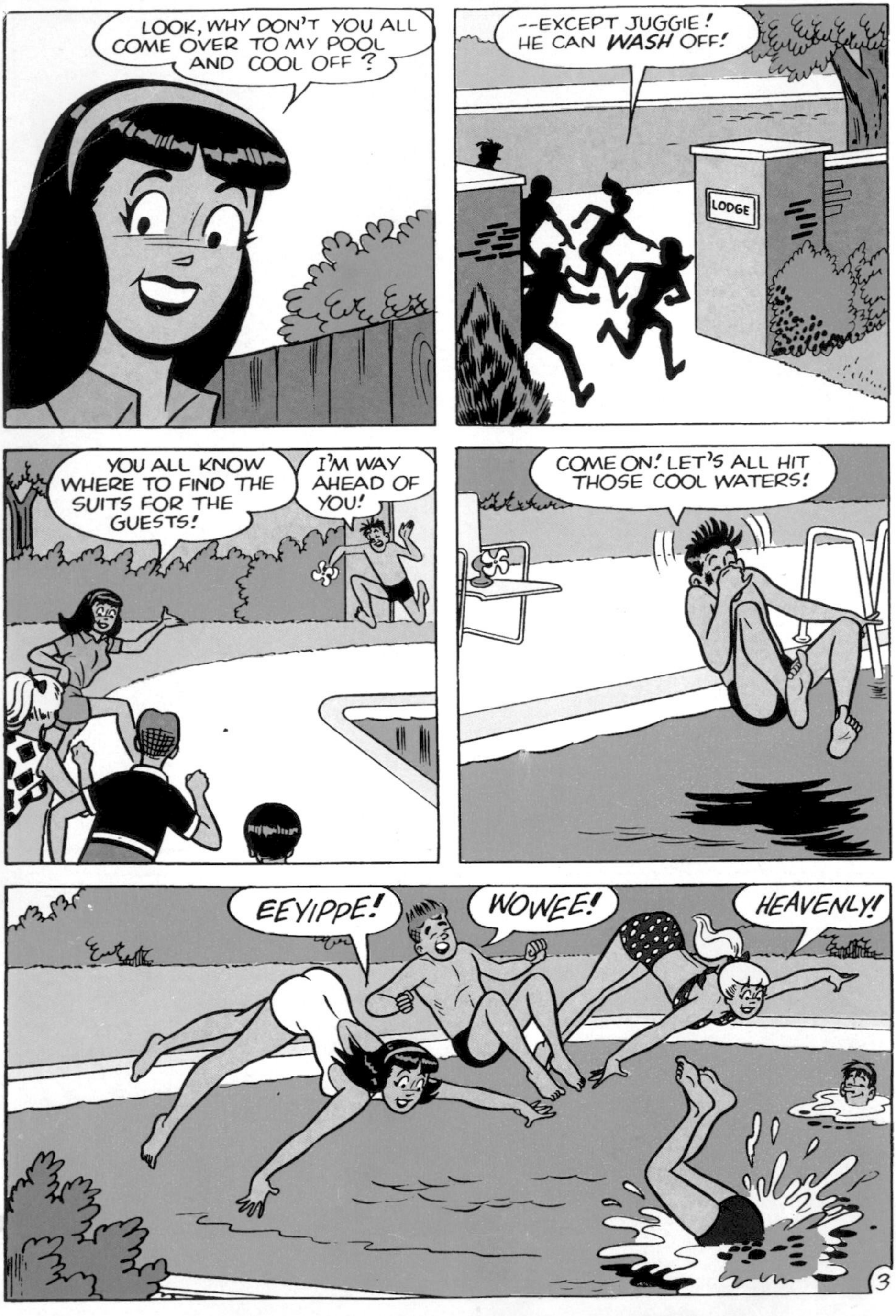
LOOK, WHY DON'T YOU ALL COME OVER TO MY POOL AND COOL OFF?
--EXCEPT JUGGIE! HE CAN WASH OFF!
LODGE
YOU ALL KNOW WHERE TO FIND THE SUITS FOR THE GUESTS!
I'M WAY AHEAD OF YOU!
COME ON! LET'S ALL HIT THOSE COOL WATERS!
EEYIPPE!
WOWEE!
HEAVENLY!
3

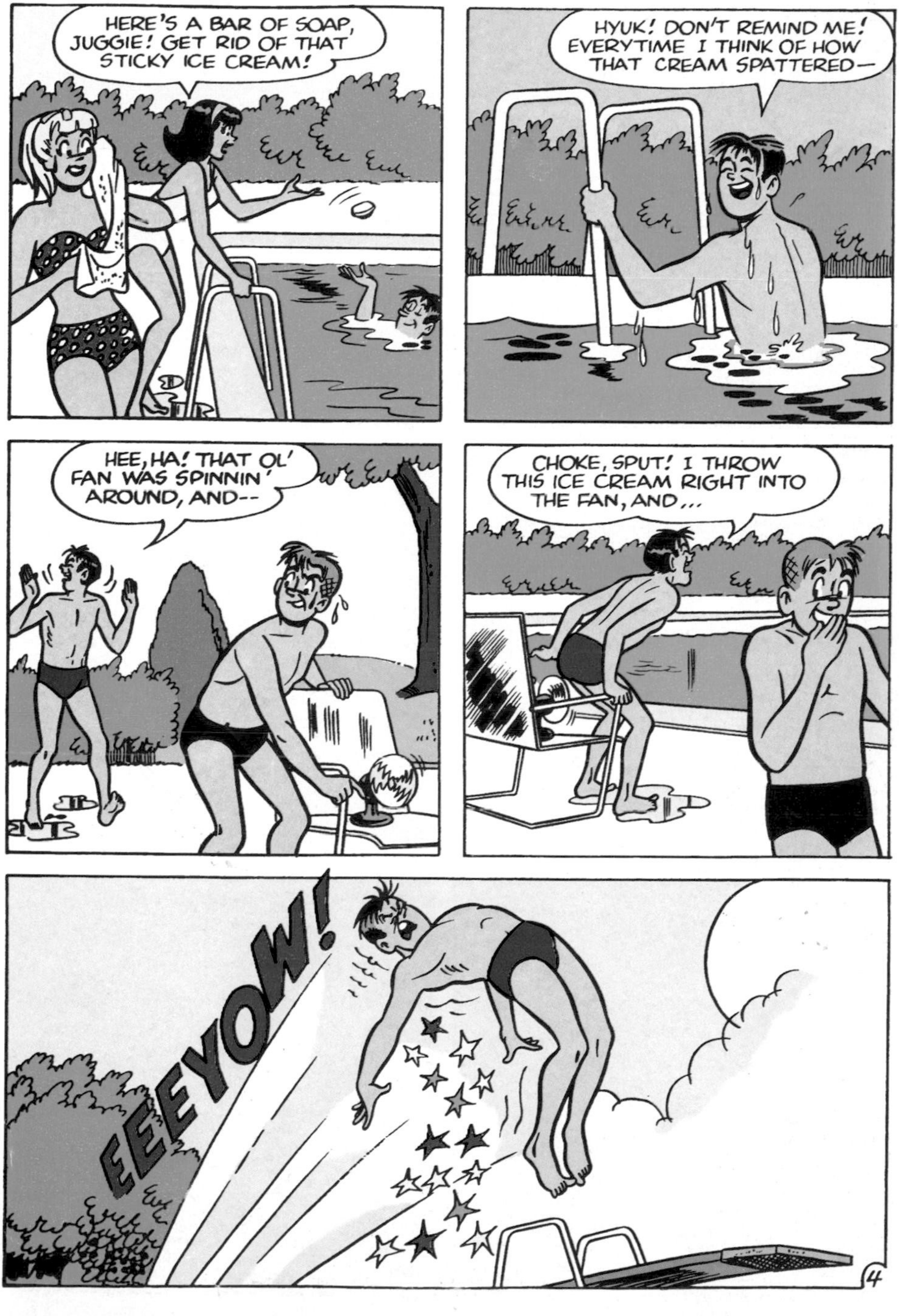
HERE'S A BAR OF SOAP, JUGGIE! GET RID OF THAT STICKY ICE CREAM!
HYUK! DON'T REMIND ME! EVERYTIME I THINK OF HOW THAT CREAM SPATTERED—
HEE, HA! THAT OL' FAN WAS SPINNIN' AROUND, AND--
CHOKE, SPUT! I THROW THIS ICE CREAM RIGHT INTO THE FAN, AND...
EEEYOW!
4

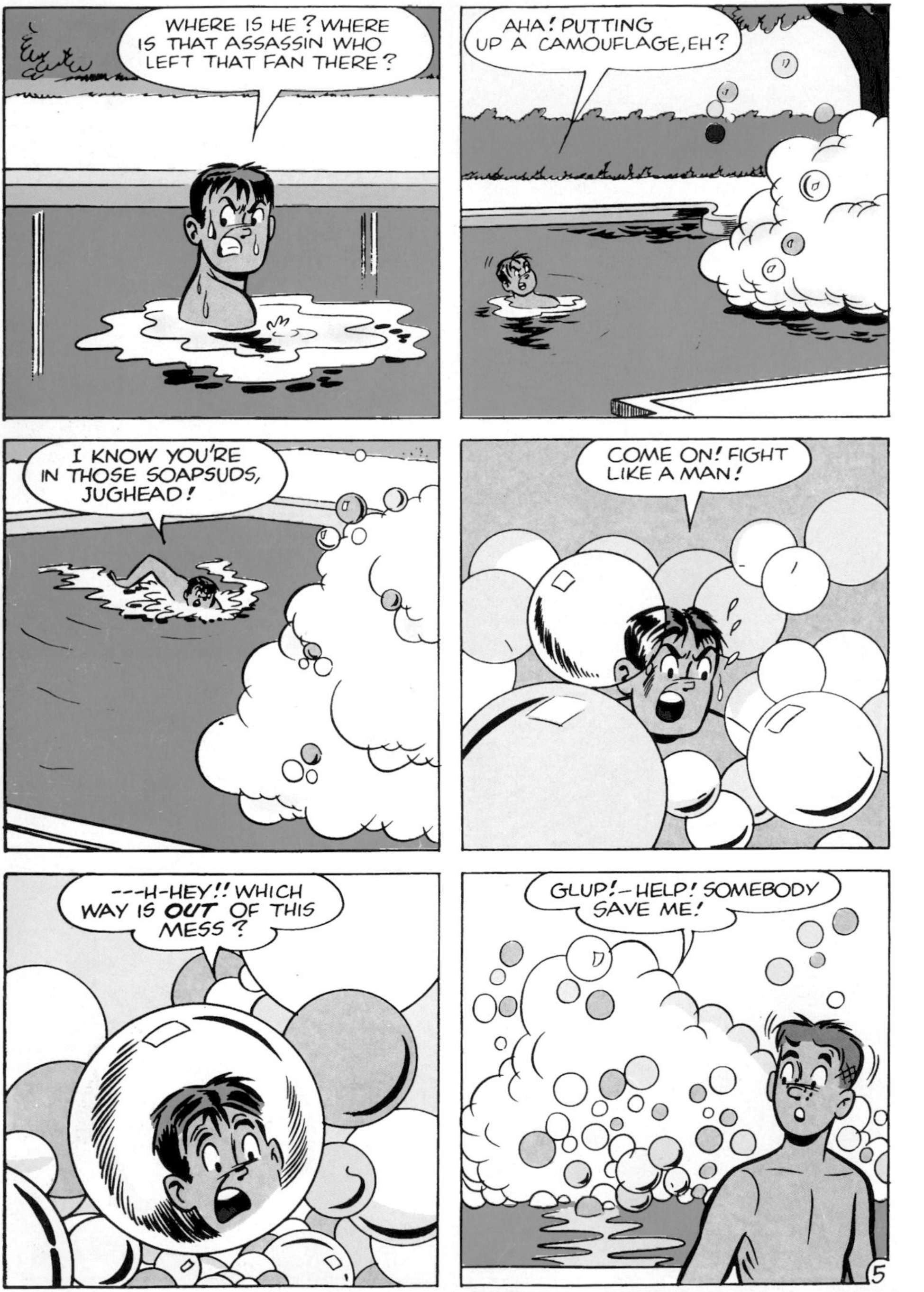
WHERE IS HE? WHERE IS THAT ASSASSIN WHO LEFT THAT FAN THERE?
AHA! PUTTING UP A CAMOUFLAGE, EH?
I KNOW YOU'RE IN THOSE SOAPSUDS, JUGHEAD!
COME ON! FIGHT LIKE A MAN!
---H-HEY!! WHICH WAY IS OUT OF THIS MESS?
GLUP!-HELP! SOMEBODY SAVE ME!
5

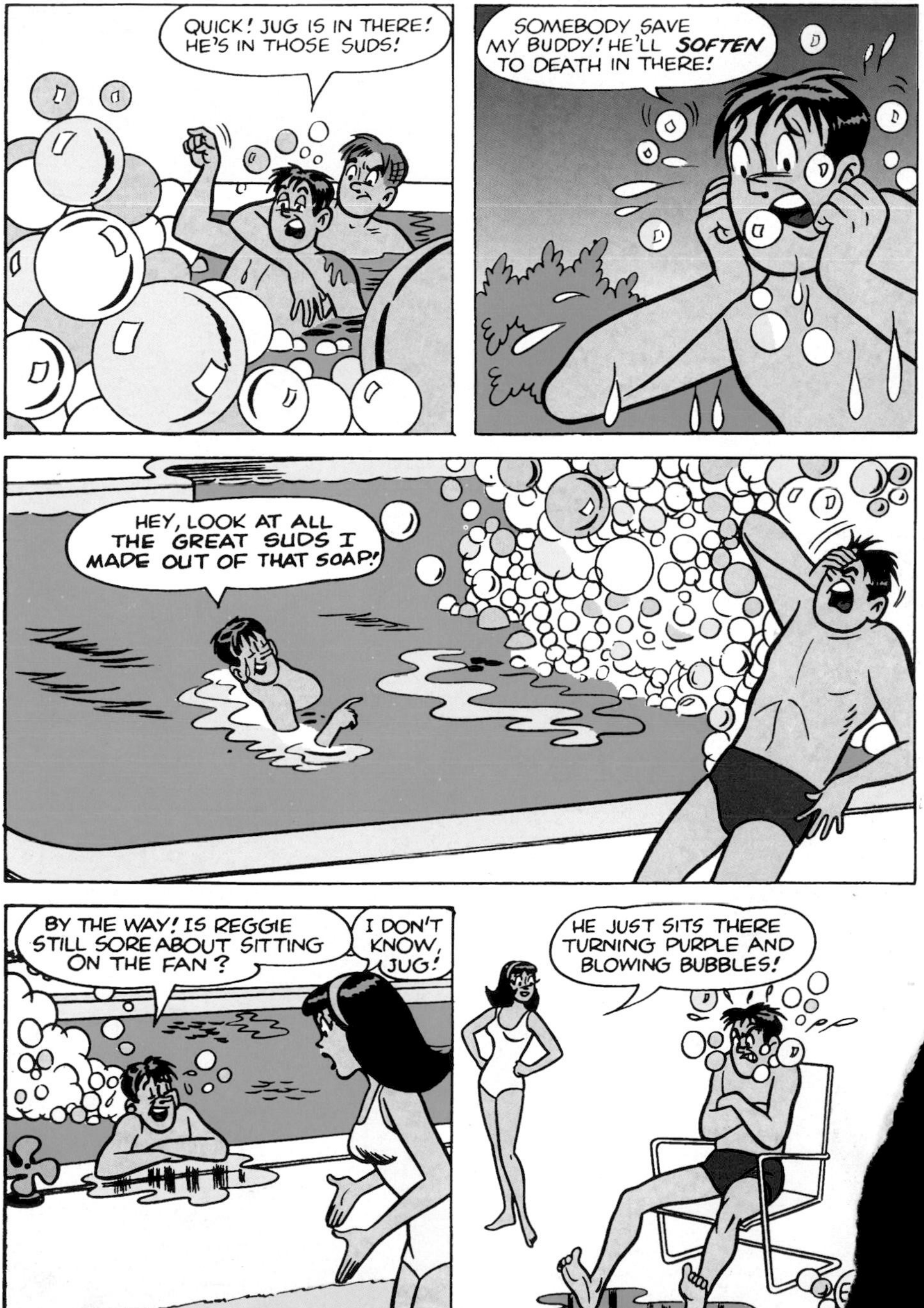
QUICK! JUG IS IN THERE! HE'S IN THOSE SUDS!
SOMEBODY SAVE MY BUDDY! HE'LL SOFTEN TO DEATH IN THERE!
HEY, LOOK AT ALL THE GREAT SUDS I MADE OUT OF THAT SOAP!
BY THE WAY! IS REGGIE STILL SORE ABOUT SITTING ON THE FAN?
I DON'T KNOW, JUG!
HE JUST SITS THERE TURNING PURPLE AND BLOWING BUBBLES!

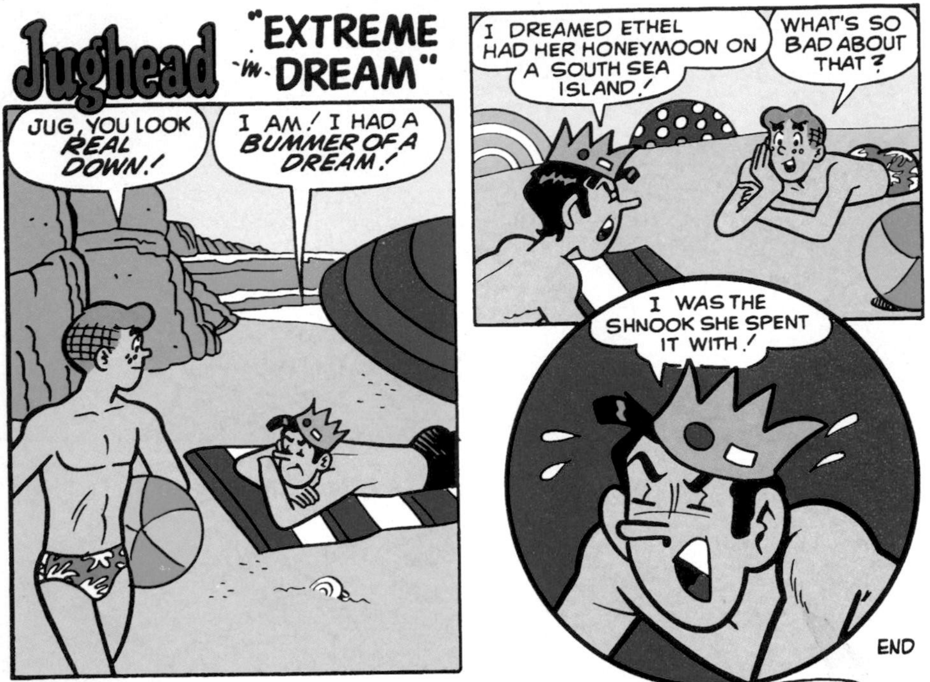
Jughead
"EXTREME in DREAM"
JUG, YOU LOOK REAL DOWN!
I AM! I HAD A BUMMER OF A DREAM!
I DREAMED ETHEL HAD HER HONEYMOON ON A SOUTH SEA ISLAND!
WHAT'S SO BAD ABOUT THAT?
I WAS THE SHNOOK SHE SPENT IT WITH!
END

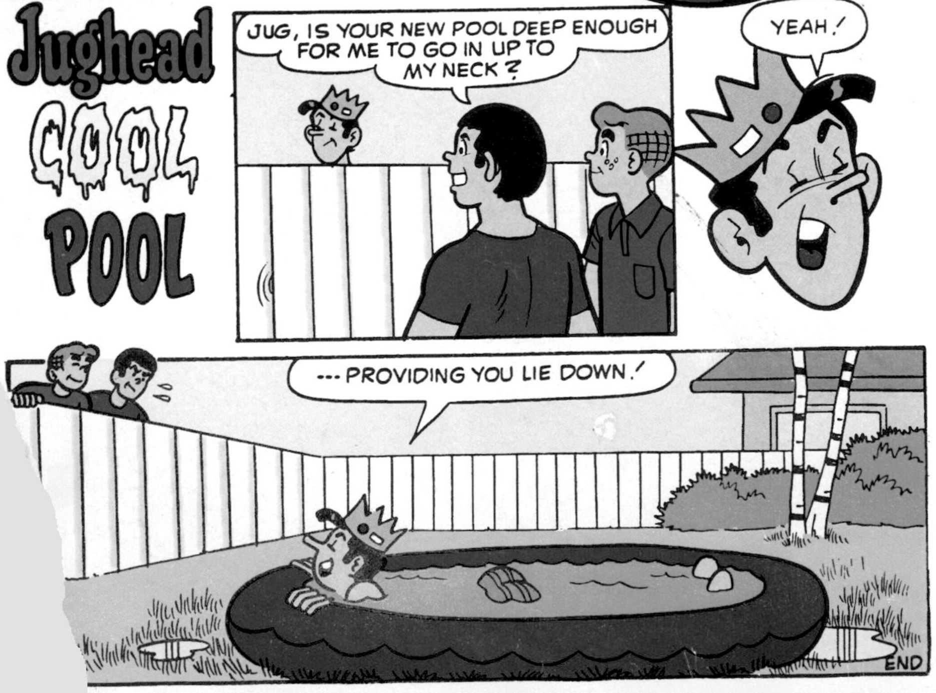
Jughead
COOL POOL
JUG, IS YOUR NEW POOL DEEP ENOUGH FOR ME TO GO IN UP TO MY NECK?
YEAH!
--- PROVIDING YOU LIE DOWN!
END

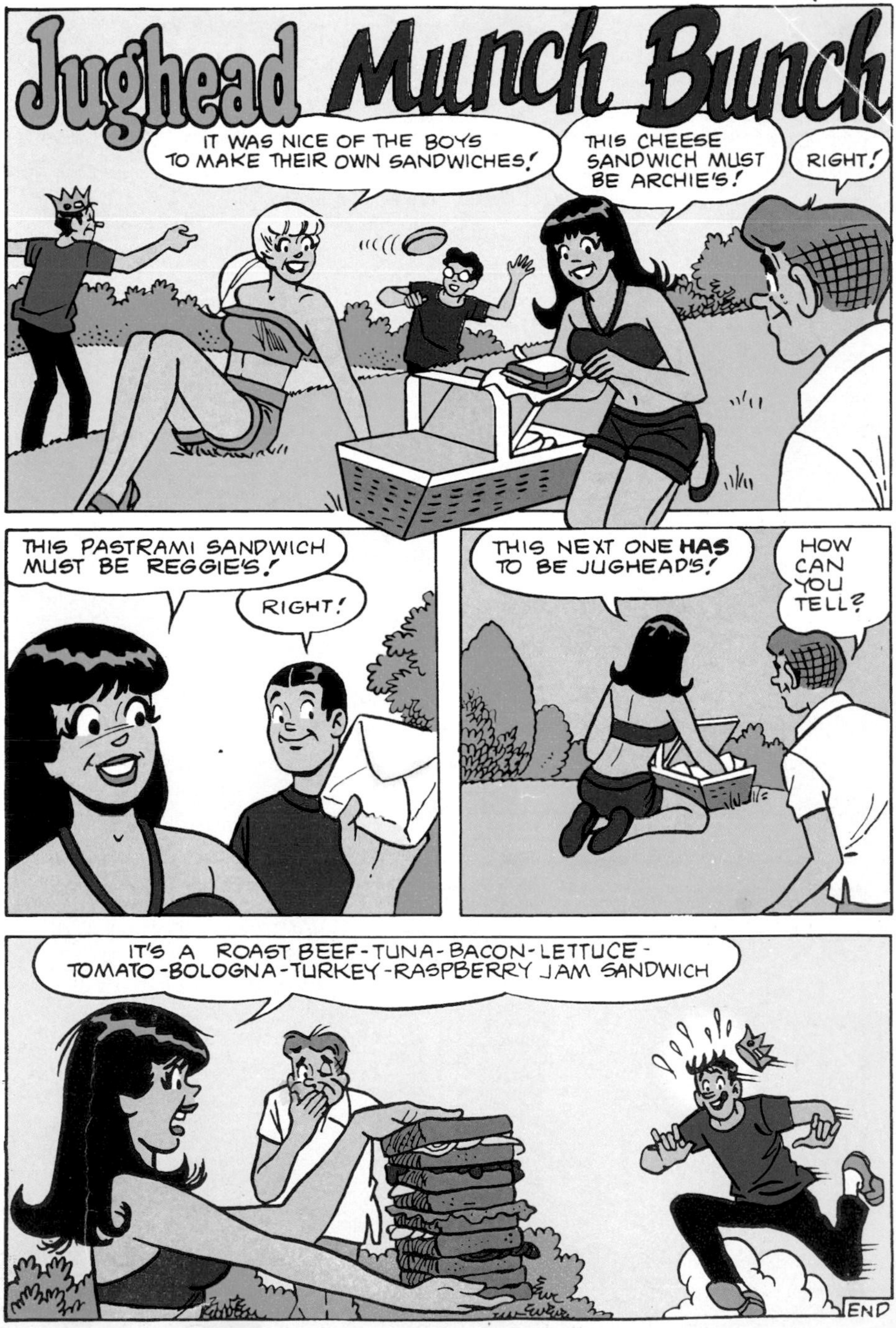
Jughead
Munch Bunch
IT WAS NICE OF THE BOYS TO MAKE THEIR OWN SANDWICHES!
THIS CHEESE SANDWICH MUST BE ARCHIE'S!
RIGHT!
THIS PASTRAMI SANDWICH MUST BE REGGIE'S!
RIGHT!
THIS NEXT ONE **HAS** TO BE JUGHEAD'S!
HOW CAN YOU TELL?
IT'S A ROAST BEEF-TUNA-BACON-LETTUCE-TOMATO-BOLOGNA-TURKEY-RASPBERRY JAM SANDWICH
END

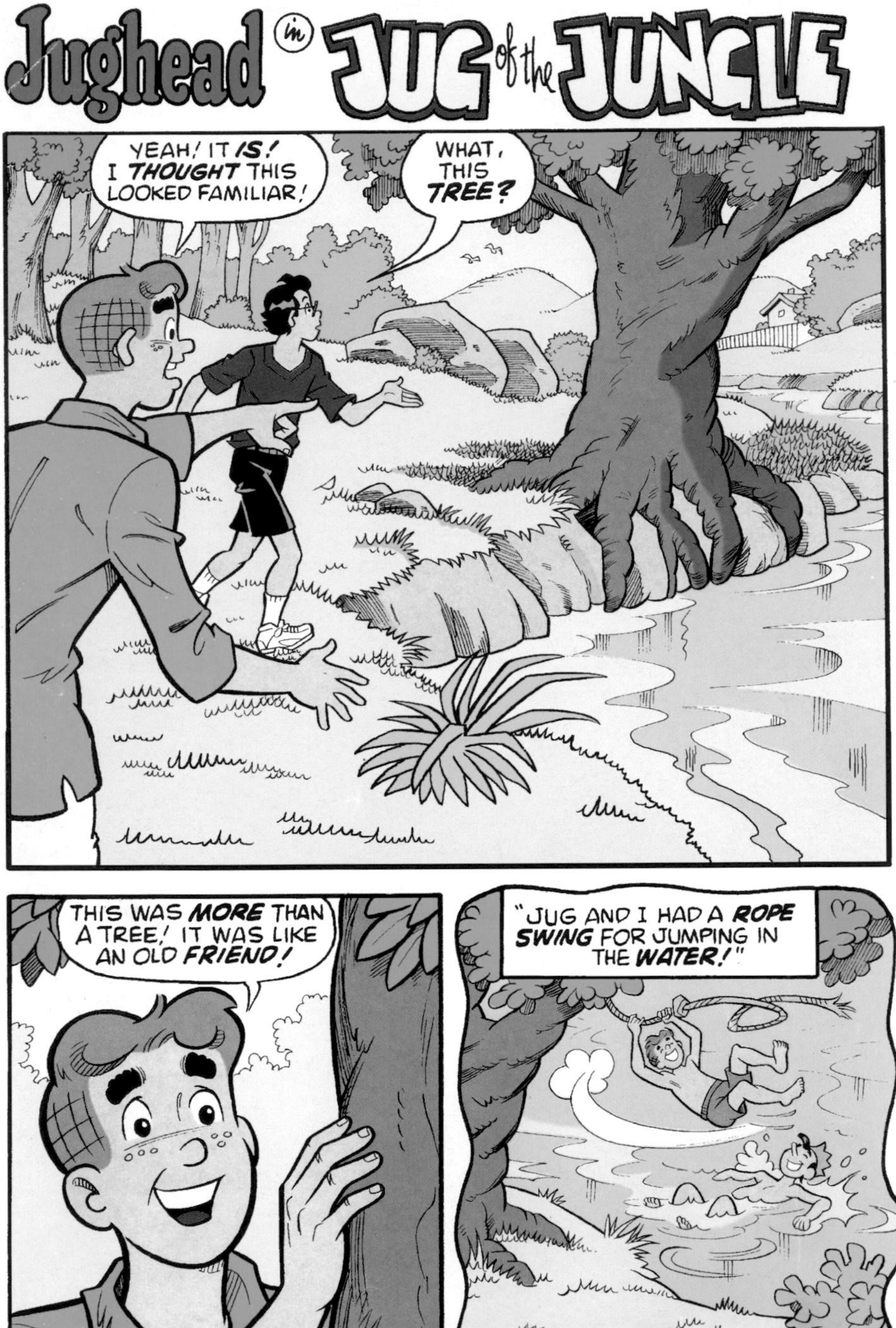
Jughead in JUG of the JUNGLE
YEAH! IT IS! I THOUGHT THIS LOOKED FAMILIAR!
WHAT, THIS TREE?
THIS WAS MORE THAN A TREE! IT WAS LIKE AN OLD FRIEND!
"JUG AND I HAD A ROPE SWING FOR JUMPING IN THE WATER!"

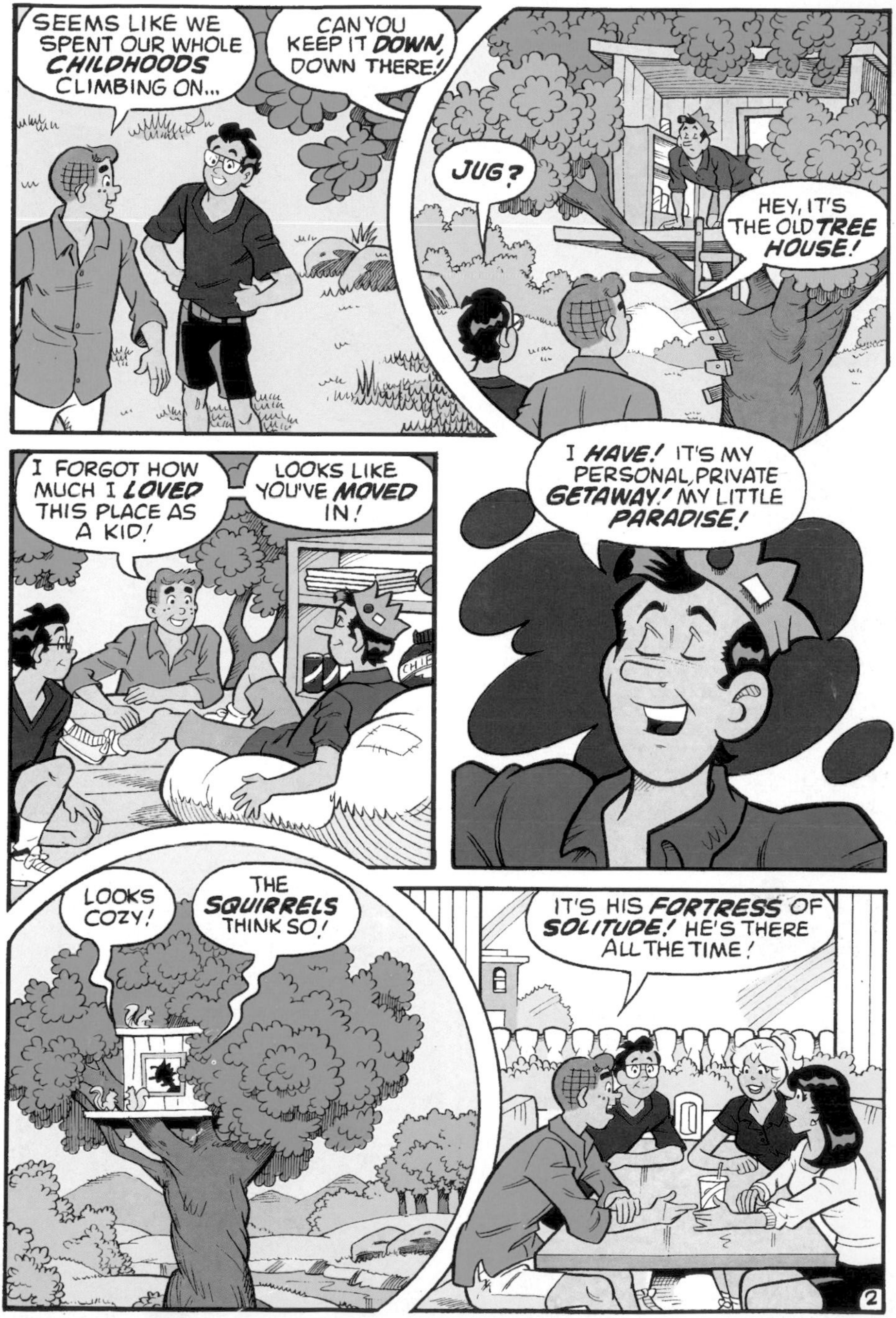
SEEMS LIKE WE SPENT OUR WHOLE CHILDHOODS CLIMBING ON...
CAN YOU KEEP IT DOWN, DOWN THERE!
JUG?
HEY, IT'S THE OLD TREE HOUSE!
I FORGOT HOW MUCH I LOVED THIS PLACE AS A KID!
LOOKS LIKE YOU'VE MOVED IN!
I HAVE! IT'S MY PERSONAL, PRIVATE GETAWAY! MY LITTLE PARADISE!
LOOKS COZY!
THE SQUIRRELS THINK SO!
IT'S HIS FORTRESS OF SOLITUDE! HE'S THERE ALL THE TIME!
2

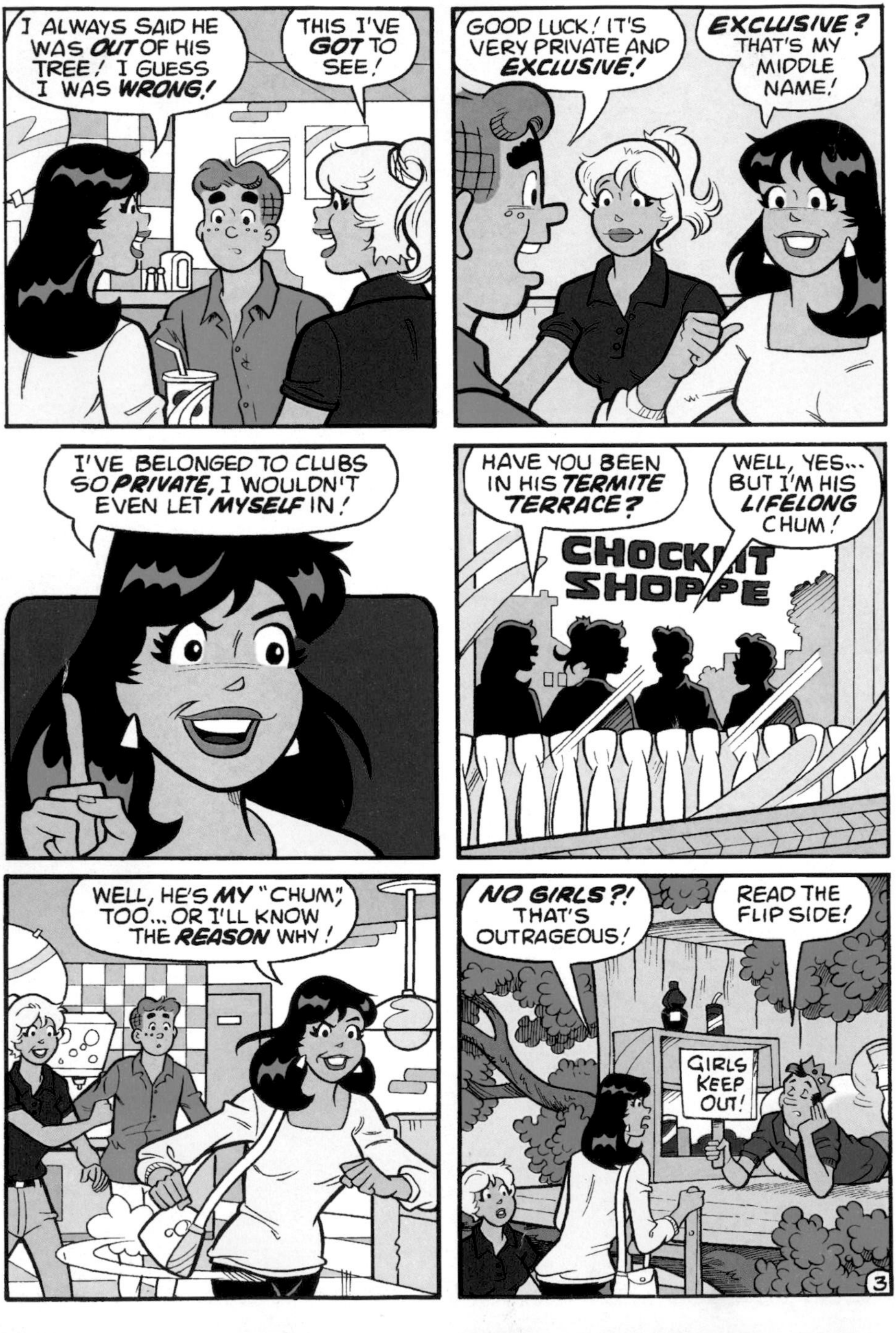
I ALWAYS SAID HE WAS OUT OF HIS TREE! I GUESS I WAS WRONG!
THIS I'VE GOT TO SEE!
GOOD LUCK! IT'S VERY PRIVATE AND EXCLUSIVE!
EXCLUSIVE? THAT'S MY MIDDLE NAME!
I'VE BELONGED TO CLUBS SO PRIVATE, I WOULDN'T EVEN LET MYSELF IN!
HAVE YOU BEEN IN HIS TERMITE TERRACE?
WELL, YES... BUT I'M HIS LIFELONG CHUM!
CHOCKLIT SHOPPE
WELL, HE'S MY "CHUM," TOO... OR I'LL KNOW THE REASON WHY!
NO GIRLS?! THAT'S OUTRAGEOUS!
READ THE FLIP SIDE!
GIRLS KEEP OUT!
3

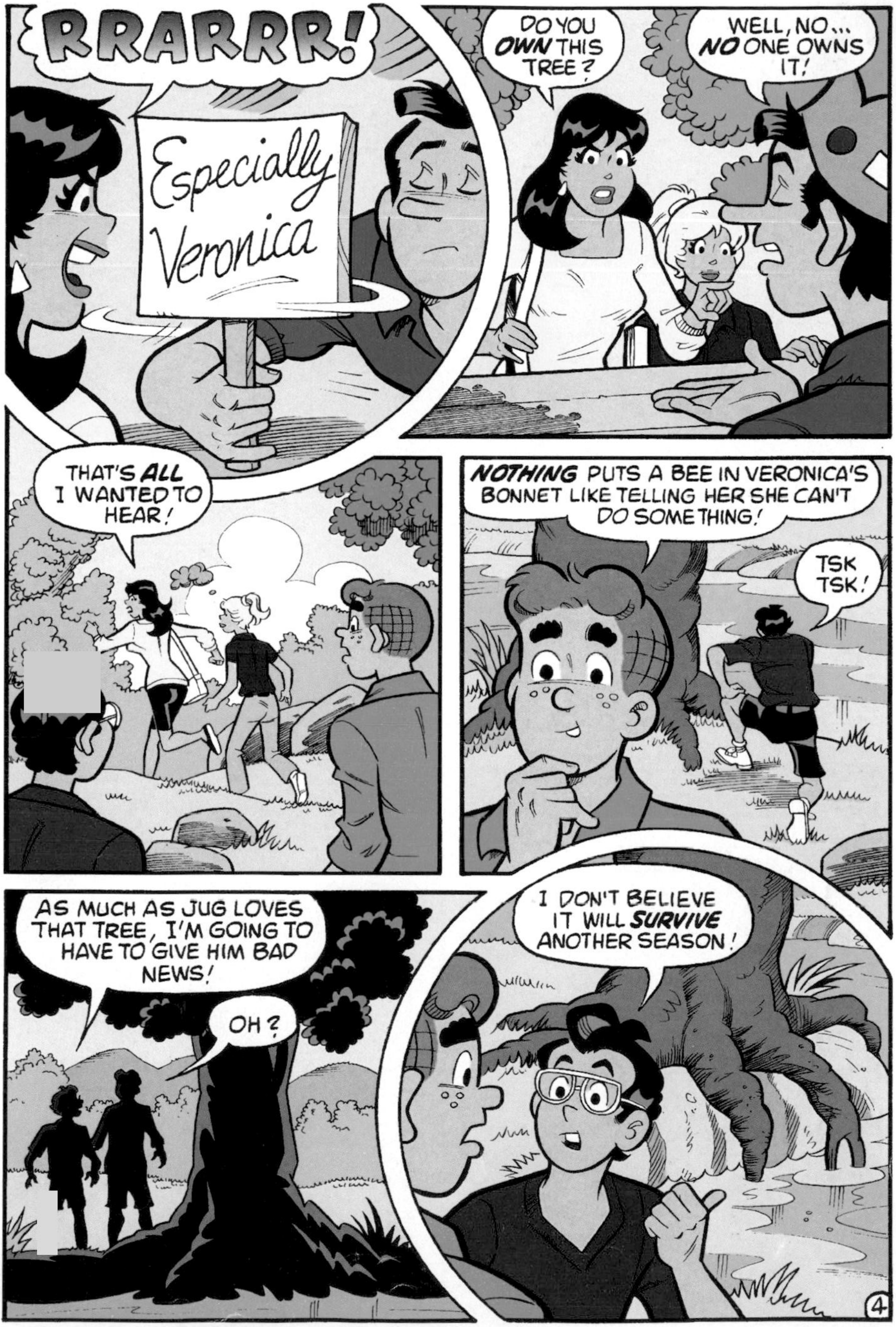
RRARRR!
Especially Veronica
DO YOU OWN THIS TREE?
WELL, NO... NO ONE OWNS IT!
THAT'S ALL I WANTED TO HEAR!
NOTHING PUTS A BEE IN VERONICA'S BONNET LIKE TELLING HER SHE CAN'T DO SOMETHING!
TSK TSK!
AS MUCH AS JUG LOVES THAT TREE, I'M GOING TO HAVE TO GIVE HIM BAD NEWS!
OH?
I DON'T BELIEVE IT WILL SURVIVE ANOTHER SEASON!
4

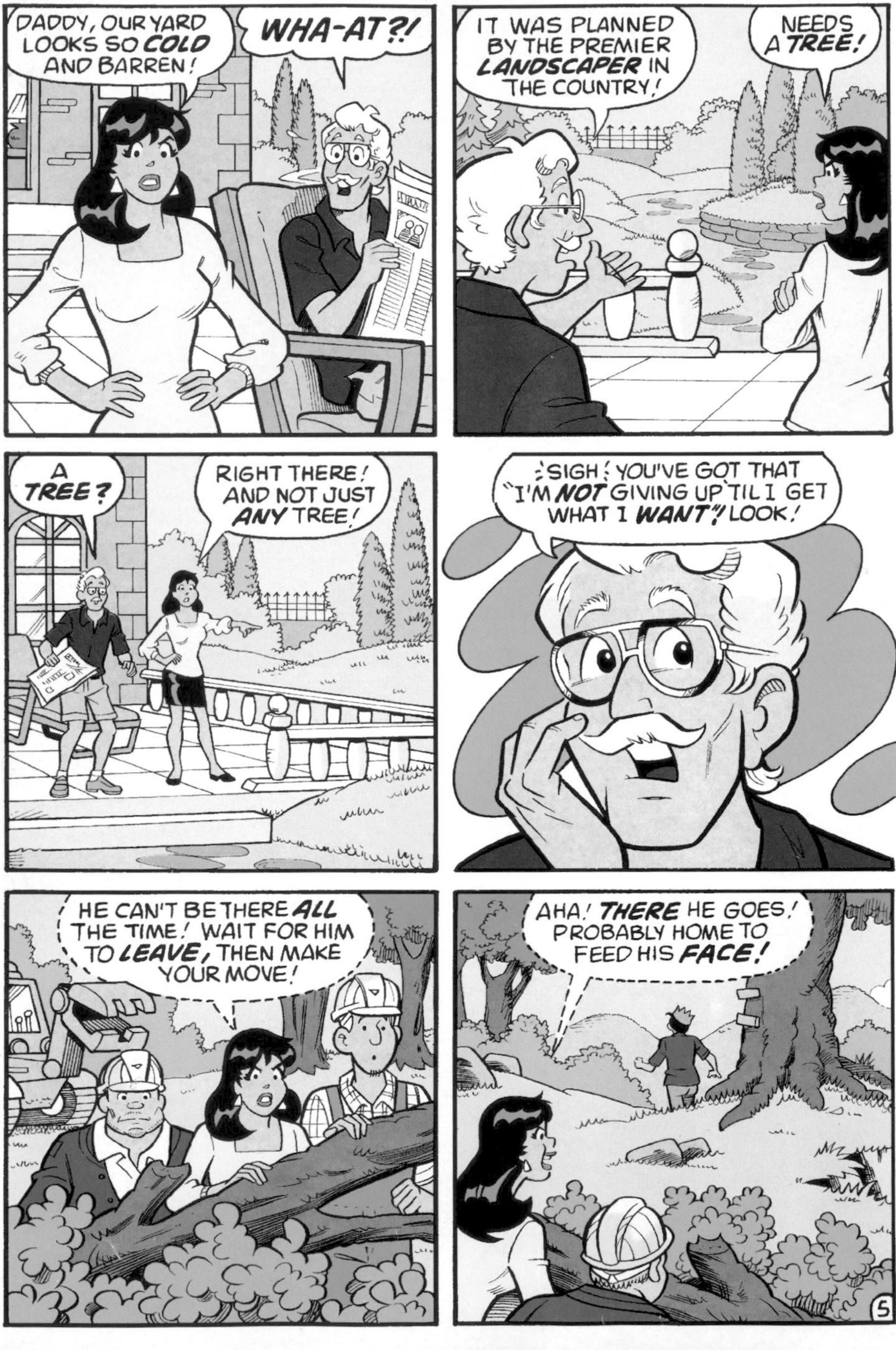
DADDY, OUR YARD LOOKS SO COLD AND BARREN!
WHA-AT?!
IT WAS PLANNED BY THE PREMIER LANDSCAPER IN THE COUNTRY!
NEEDS A TREE!
A TREE?
RIGHT THERE! AND NOT JUST ANY TREE!
SIGH! YOU'VE GOT THAT "I'M NOT GIVING UP 'TIL I GET WHAT I WANT"! LOOK!
HE CAN'T BE THERE ALL THE TIME! WAIT FOR HIM TO LEAVE, THEN MAKE YOUR MOVE!
AHA! THERE HE GOES! PROBABLY HOME TO FEED HIS FACE!
5

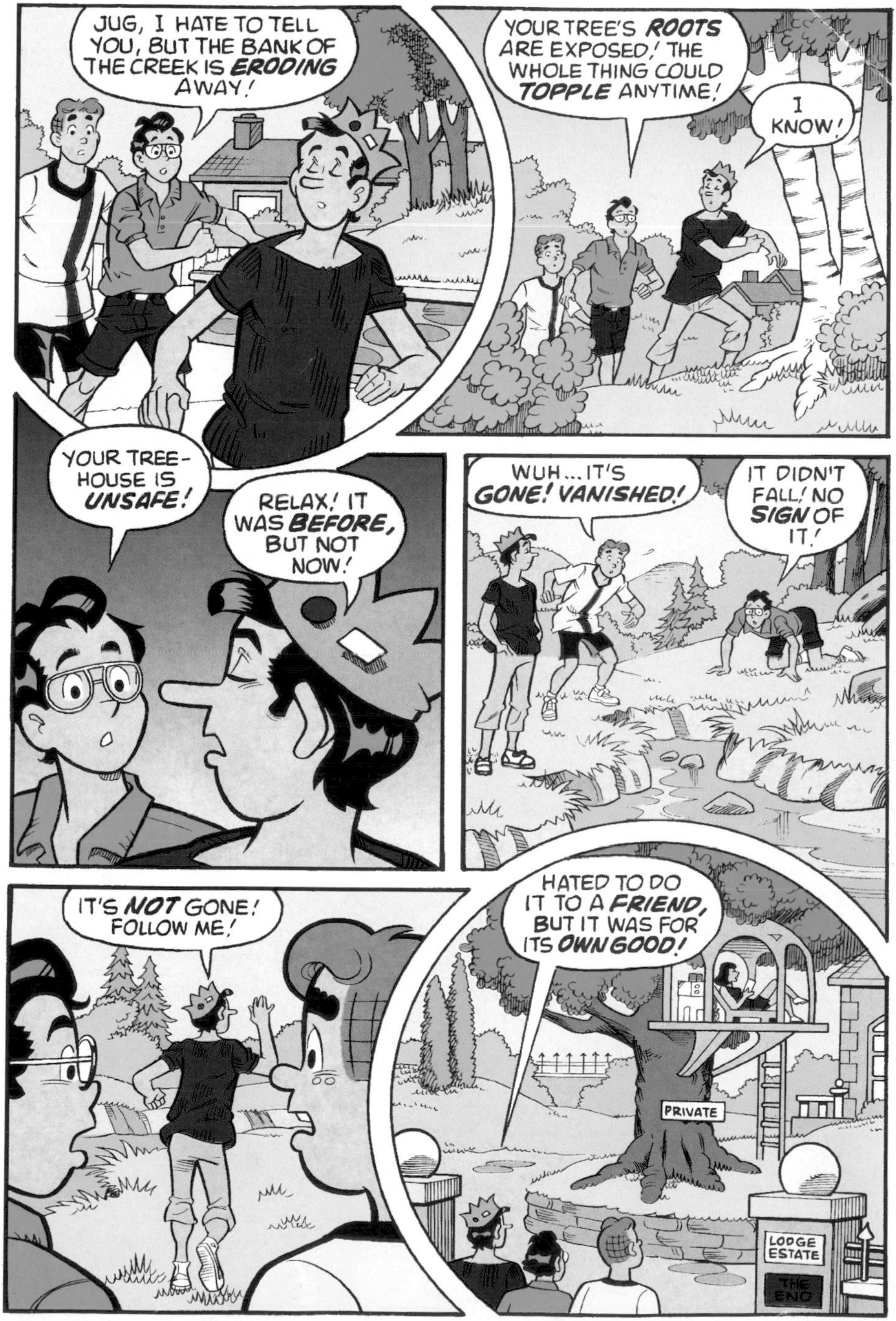
JUG, I HATE TO TELL YOU, BUT THE BANK OF THE CREEK IS ERODING AWAY!
YOUR TREE'S ROOTS ARE EXPOSED! THE WHOLE THING COULD TOPPLE ANYTIME!
I KNOW!
YOUR TREE-HOUSE IS UNSAFE!
RELAX! IT WAS BEFORE, BUT NOT NOW!
WUH... IT'S GONE! VANISHED!
IT DIDN'T FALL! NO SIGN OF IT!
IT'S NOT GONE! FOLLOW ME!
HATED TO DO IT TO A FRIEND, BUT IT WAS FOR ITS OWN GOOD!
PRIVATE
LODGE ESTATE
THE END

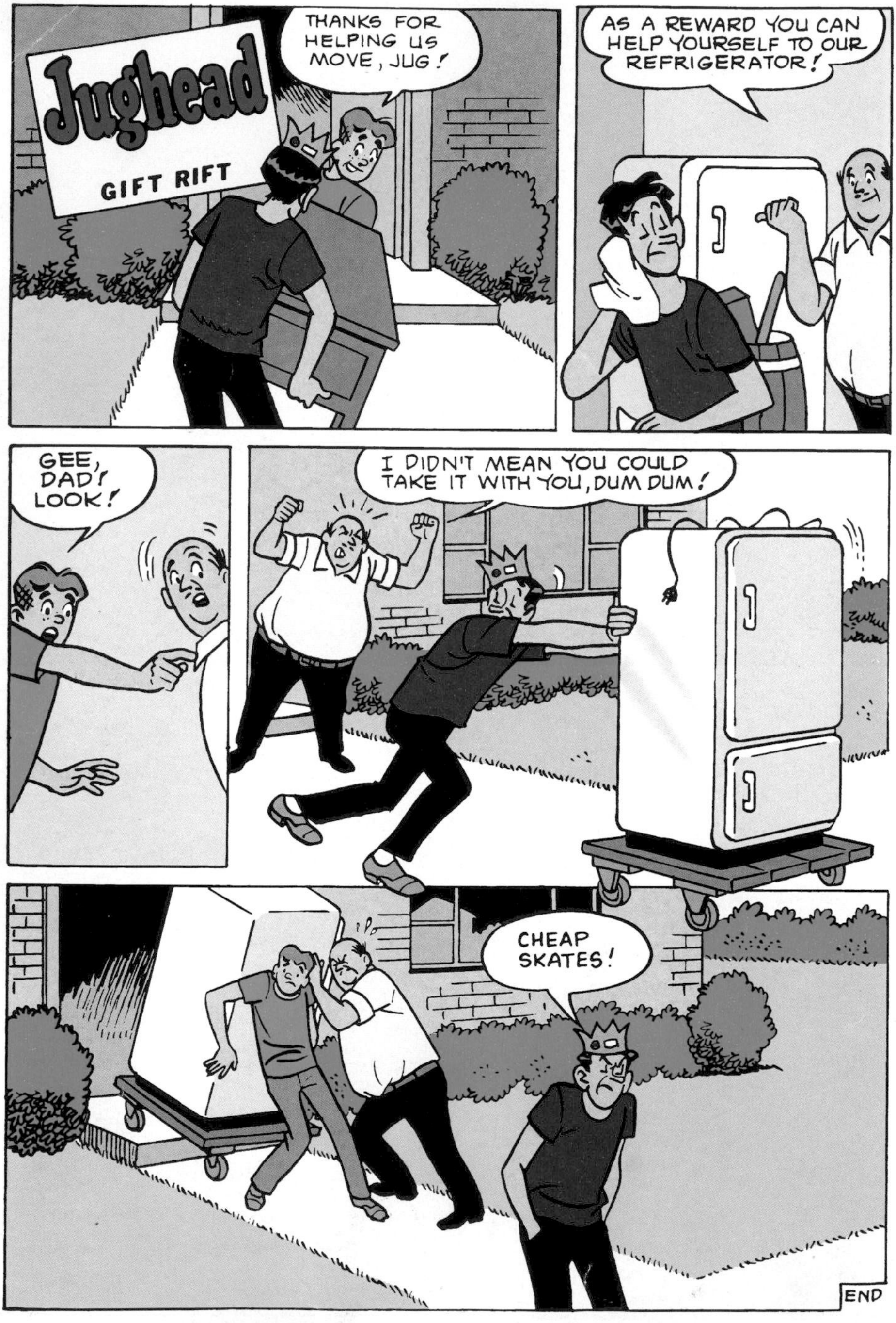
Jughead
GIFT RIFT
THANKS FOR HELPING US MOVE, JUG!
AS A REWARD YOU CAN HELP YOURSELF TO OUR REFRIGERATOR!
GEE, DAD! LOOK!
I DIDN'T MEAN YOU COULD TAKE IT WITH YOU, DUM DUM!
CHEAP SKATES!
END

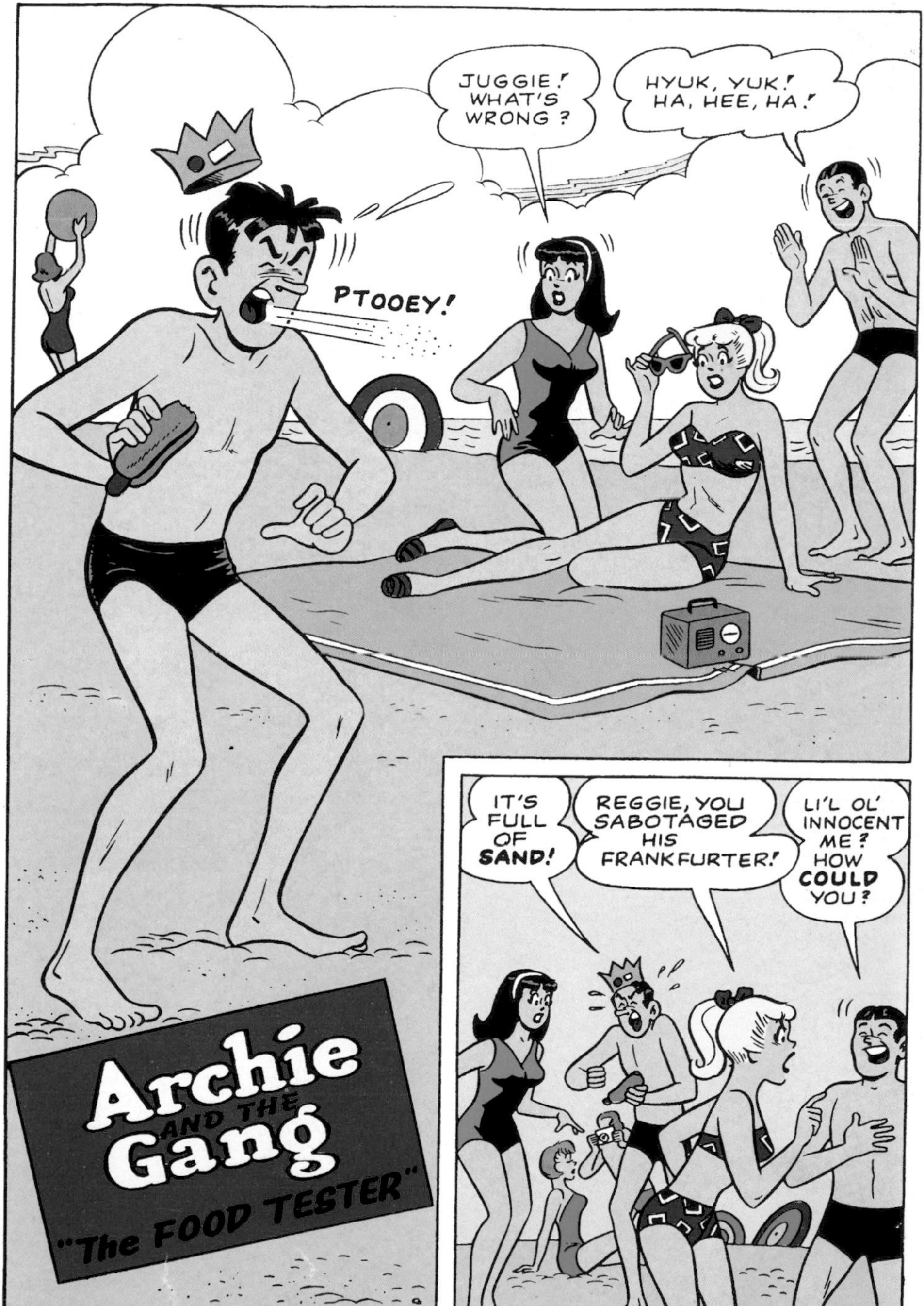
JUGGIE! WHAT'S WRONG?
HYUK, YUK! HA, HEE, HA!
PTOOEY!
Archie AND THE Gang
"The FOOD TESTER"
IT'S FULL OF SAND!
REGGIE, YOU SABOTAGED HIS FRANKFURTER!
LI'L OL' INNOCENT ME? HOW COULD YOU?

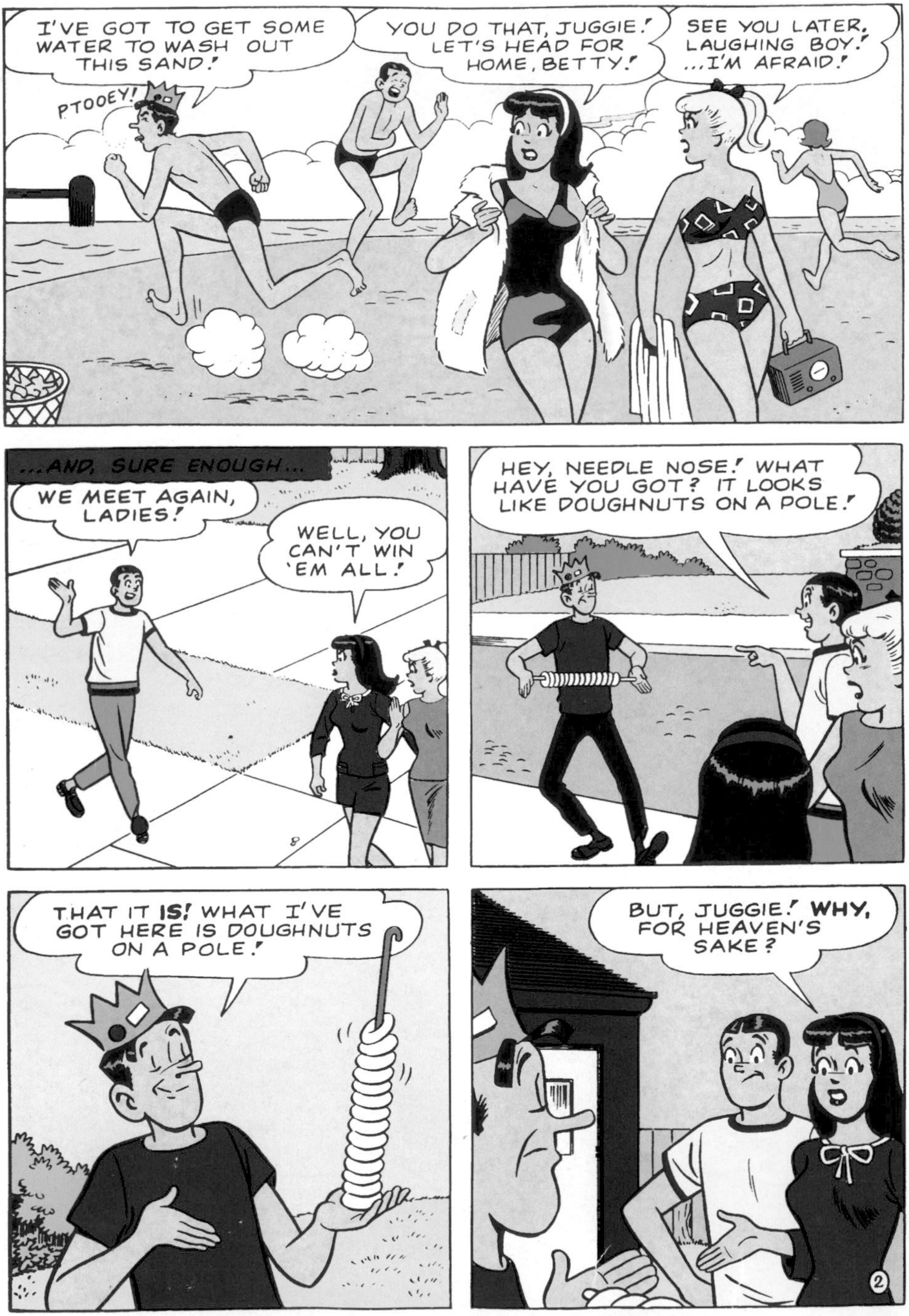
I'VE GOT TO GET SOME WATER TO WASH OUT THIS SAND!
PTOOEY!
YOU DO THAT, JUGGIE! LET'S HEAD FOR HOME, BETTY!
SEE YOU LATER, LAUGHING BOY! ...I'M AFRAID!
...AND, SURE ENOUGH...
WE MEET AGAIN, LADIES!
WELL, YOU CAN'T WIN 'EM ALL!
HEY, NEEDLE NOSE! WHAT HAVE YOU GOT? IT LOOKS LIKE DOUGHNUTS ON A POLE!
THAT IT **IS!** WHAT I'VE GOT HERE IS DOUGHNUTS ON A POLE!
BUT, JUGGIE! **WHY,** FOR HEAVEN'S SAKE?
2

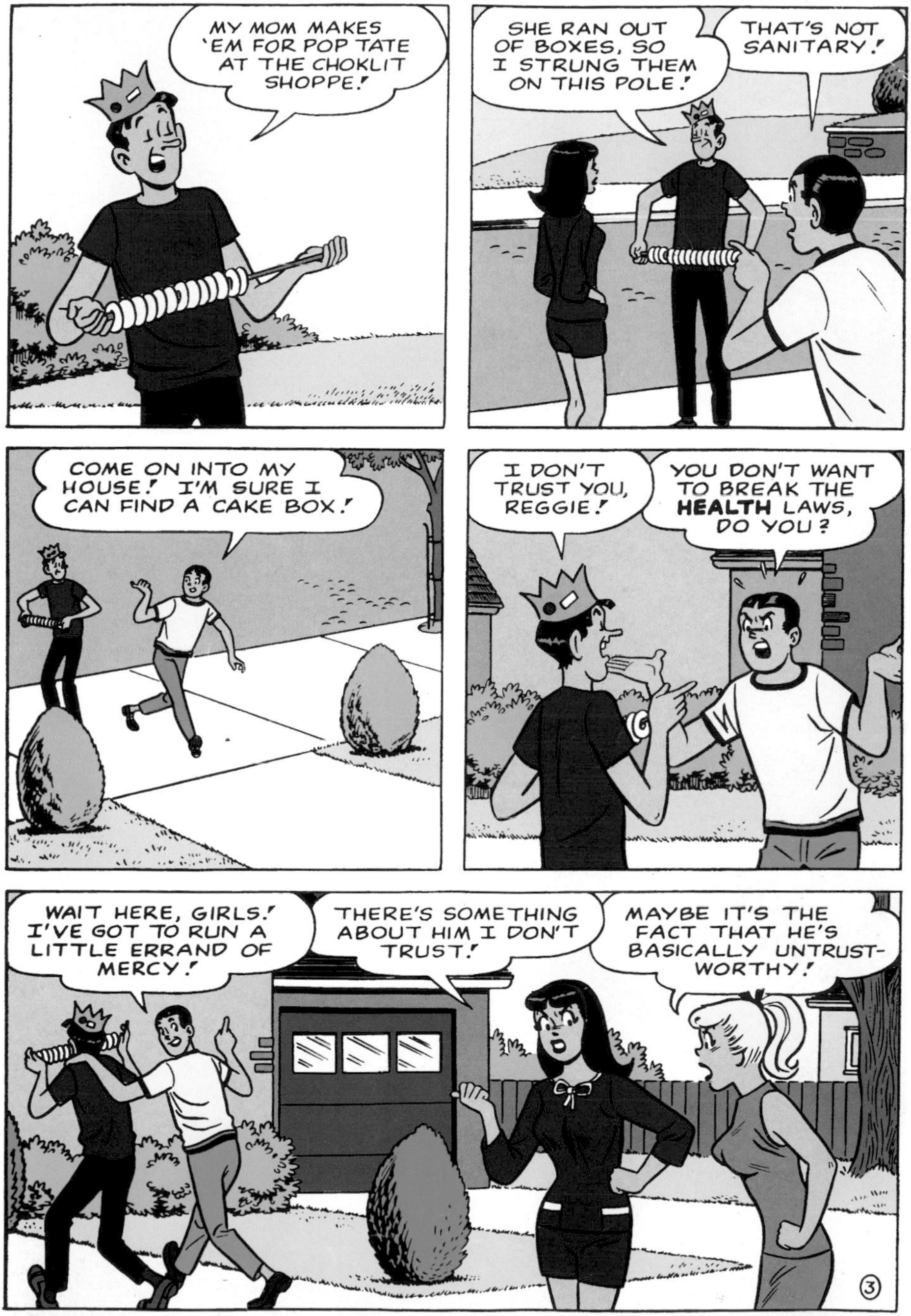
MY MOM MAKES 'EM FOR POP TATE AT THE CHOKLIT SHOPPE!
SHE RAN OUT OF BOXES, SO I STRUNG THEM ON THIS POLE!
THAT'S NOT SANITARY!
COME ON INTO MY HOUSE! I'M SURE I CAN FIND A CAKE BOX!
I DON'T TRUST YOU, REGGIE!
YOU DON'T WANT TO BREAK THE **HEALTH** LAWS, DO YOU?
WAIT HERE, GIRLS! I'VE GOT TO RUN A LITTLE ERRAND OF MERCY!
THERE'S SOMETHING ABOUT HIM I DON'T TRUST!
MAYBE IT'S THE FACT THAT HE'S BASICALLY UNTRUST-WORTHY!
3

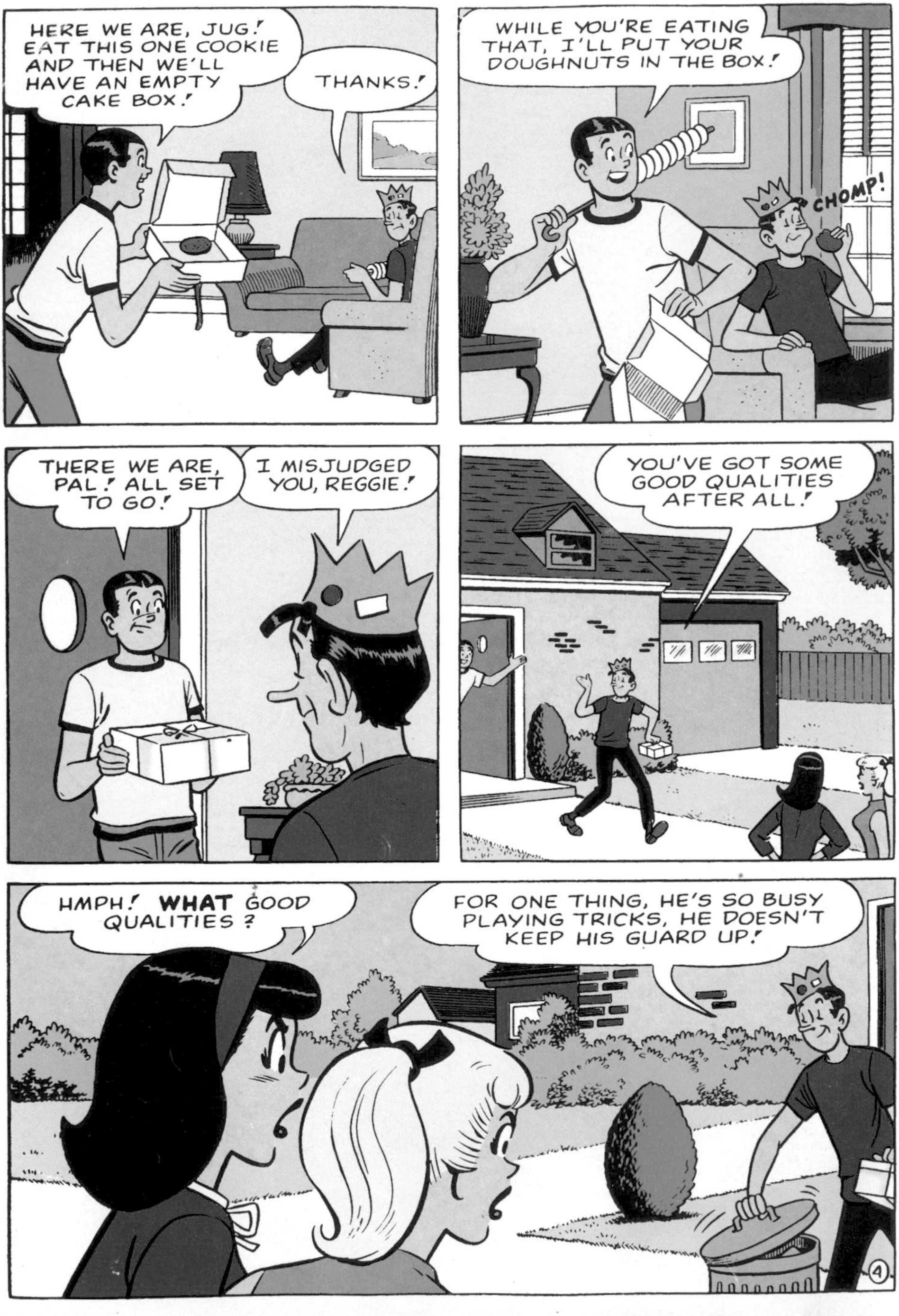
HERE WE ARE, JUG! EAT THIS ONE COOKIE AND THEN WE'LL HAVE AN EMPTY CAKE BOX!
THANKS!
WHILE YOU'RE EATING THAT, I'LL PUT YOUR DOUGHNUTS IN THE BOX!
CHOMP!
THERE WE ARE, PAL! ALL SET TO GO!
I MISJUDGED YOU, REGGIE!
YOU'VE GOT SOME GOOD QUALITIES AFTER ALL!
HMPH! **WHAT** GOOD QUALITIES ?
FOR ONE THING, HE'S SO BUSY PLAYING TRICKS, HE DOESN'T KEEP HIS GUARD UP!
4

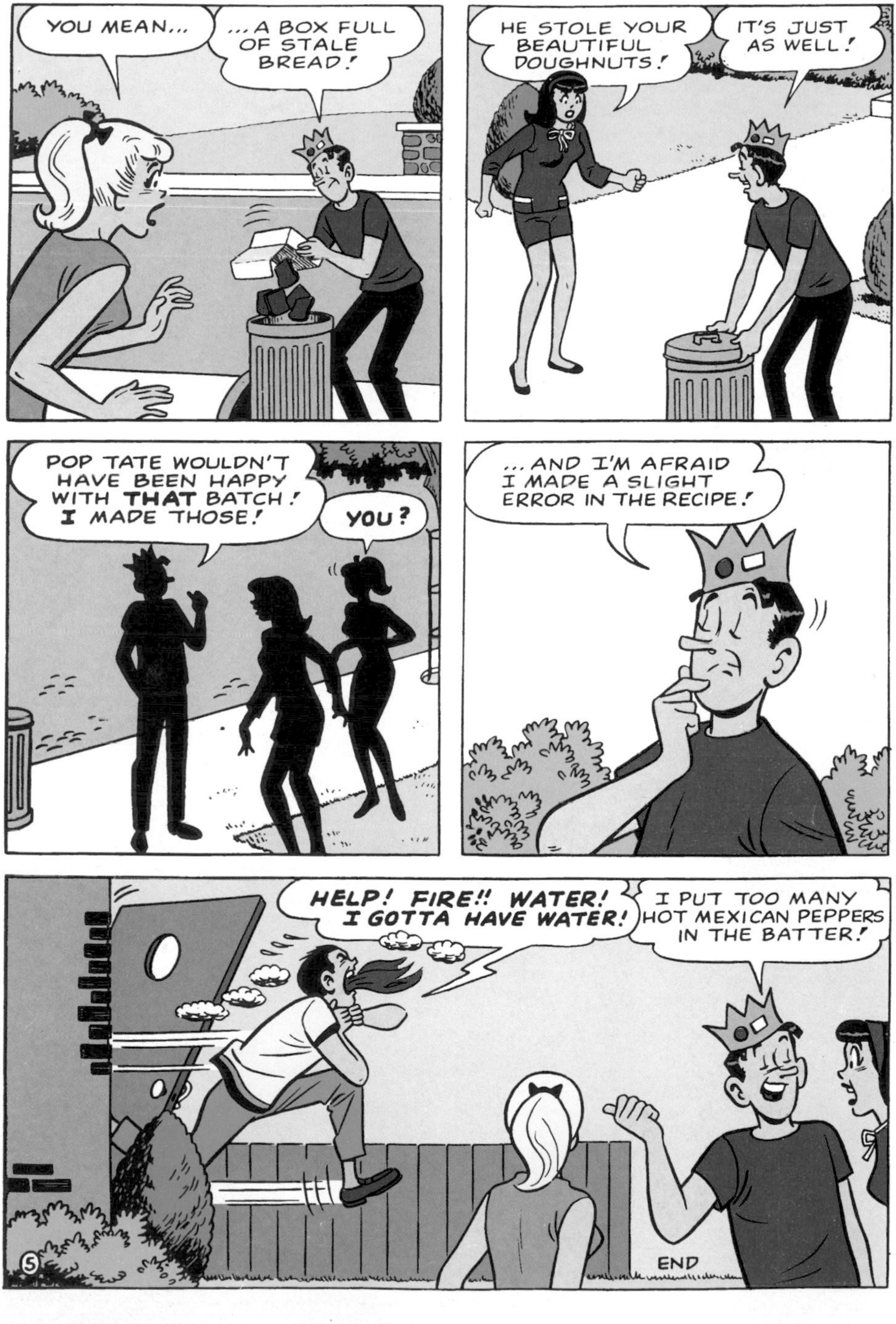
YOU MEAN...
...A BOX FULL OF STALE BREAD!
HE STOLE YOUR BEAUTIFUL DOUGHNUTS!
IT'S JUST AS WELL!
POP TATE WOULDN'T HAVE BEEN HAPPY WITH THAT BATCH! I MADE THOSE!
YOU?
...AND I'M AFRAID I MADE A SLIGHT ERROR IN THE RECIPE!
HELP! FIRE!! WATER! I GOTTA HAVE WATER!
I PUT TOO MANY HOT MEXICAN PEPPERS IN THE BATTER!
5
END

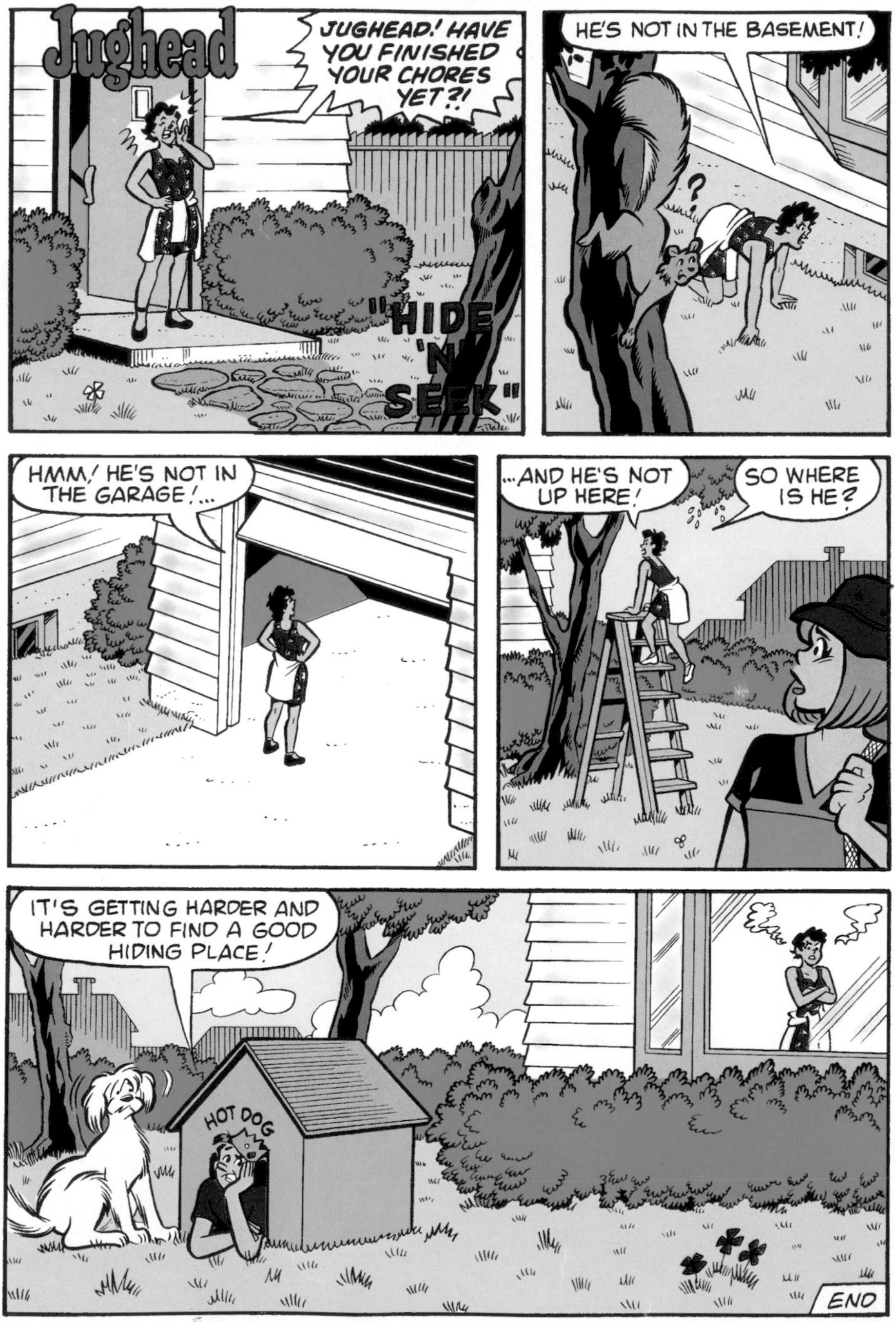
Jughead
JUGHEAD! HAVE YOU FINISHED YOUR CHORES YET?!
"HIDE 'N' SEEK"
HE'S NOT IN THE BASEMENT!
HMM! HE'S NOT IN THE GARAGE!...
...AND HE'S NOT UP HERE!
SO WHERE IS HE?
IT'S GETTING HARDER AND HARDER TO FIND A GOOD HIDING PLACE!
HOT DOG
END

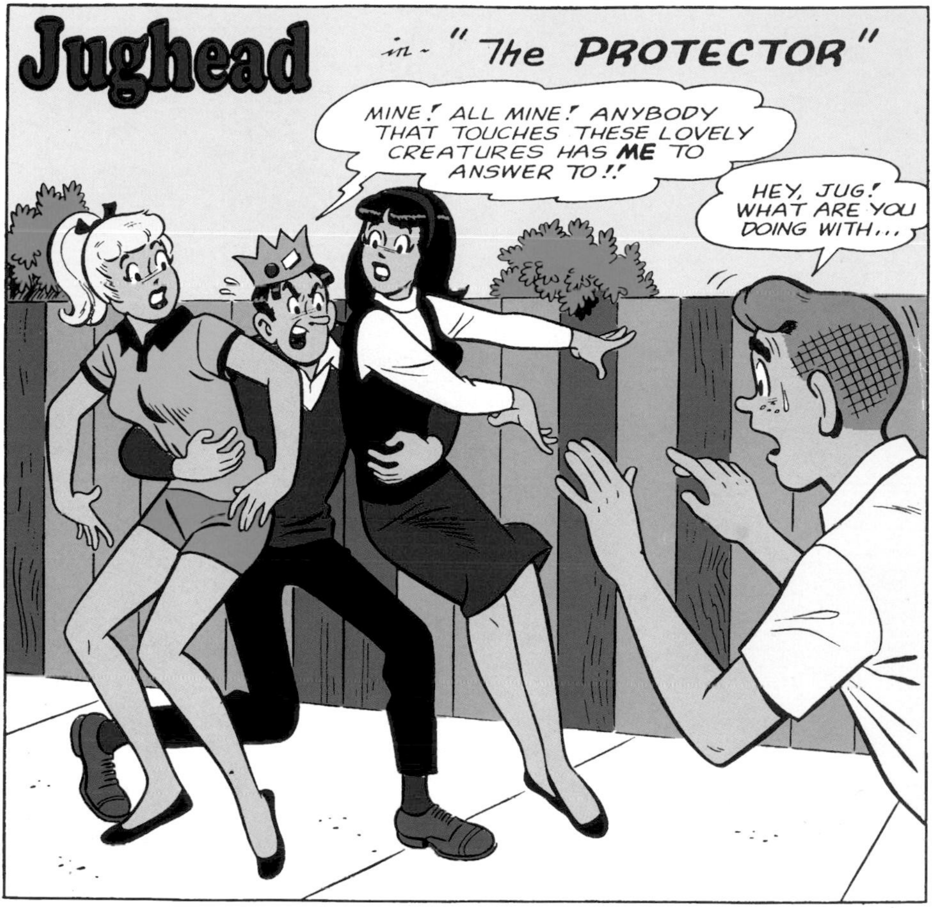
Jughead
in "The PROTECTOR"
MINE! ALL MINE! ANYBODY THAT TOUCHES THESE LOVELY CREATURES HAS ME TO ANSWER TO!!
HEY, JUG! WHAT ARE YOU DOING WITH...

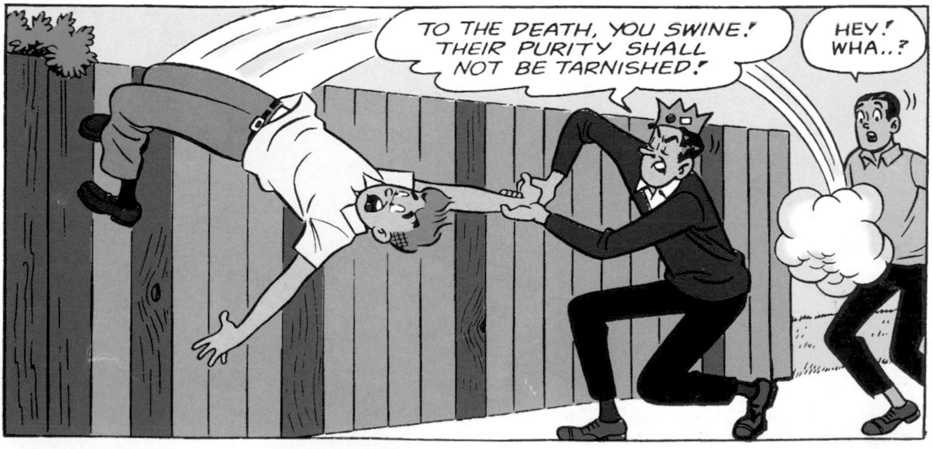
TO THE DEATH, YOU SWINE! THEIR PURITY SHALL NOT BE TARNISHED!
HEY! WHA...?

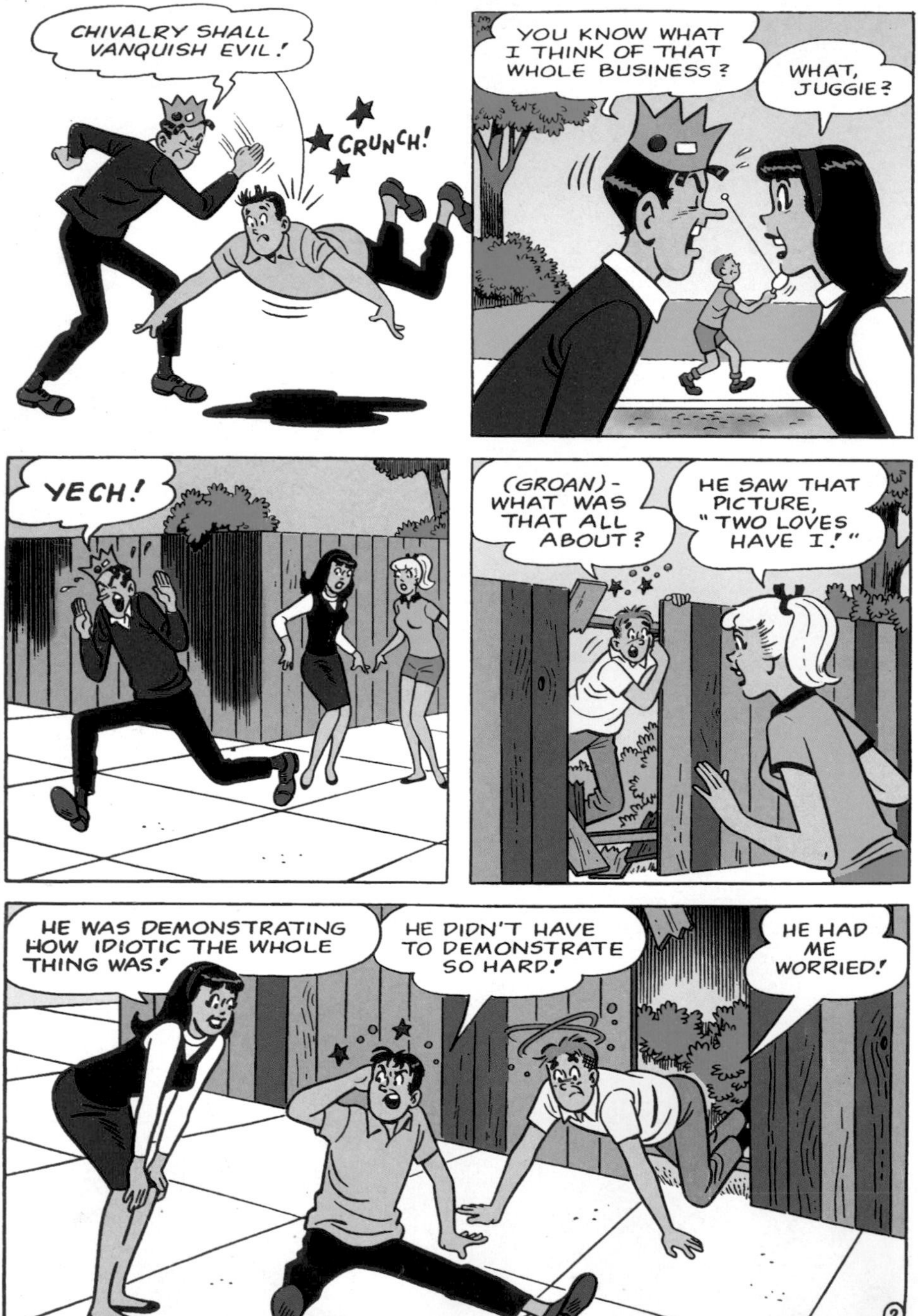
CHIVALRY SHALL VANQUISH EVIL!
CRUNCH!
YOU KNOW WHAT I THINK OF THAT WHOLE BUSINESS?
WHAT, JUGGIE?
YECH!
(GROAN)- WHAT WAS THAT ALL ABOUT?
HE SAW THAT PICTURE, "TWO LOVES HAVE I!"
HE WAS DEMONSTRATING HOW IDIOTIC THE WHOLE THING WAS!
HE DIDN'T HAVE TO DEMONSTRATE SO HARD!
HE HAD ME WORRIED!
2

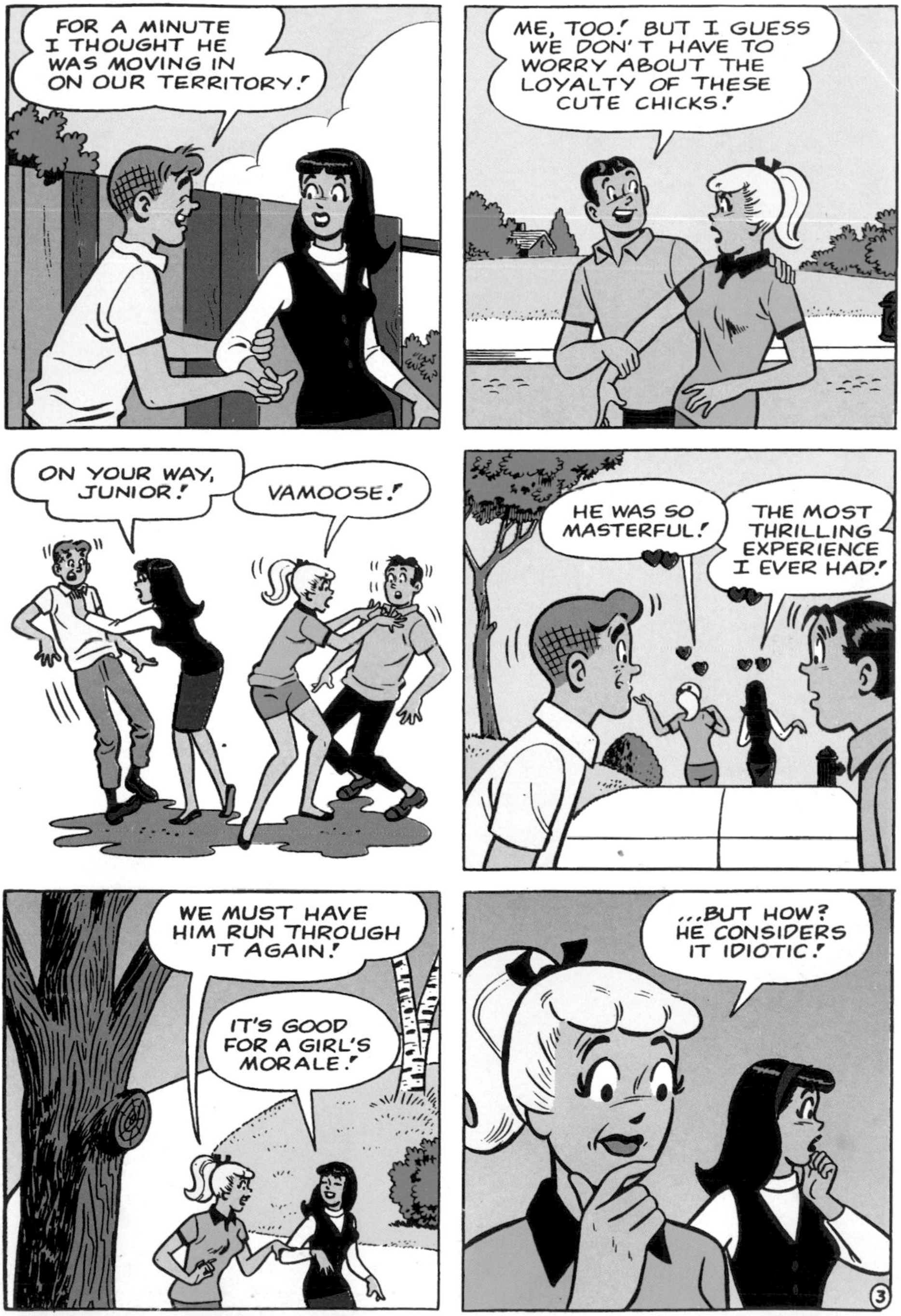
FOR A MINUTE I THOUGHT HE WAS MOVING IN ON OUR TERRITORY!
ME, TOO! BUT I GUESS WE DON'T HAVE TO WORRY ABOUT THE LOYALTY OF THESE CUTE CHICKS!
ON YOUR WAY, JUNIOR!
VAMOOSE!
HE WAS SO MASTERFUL!
THE MOST THRILLING EXPERIENCE I EVER HAD!
WE MUST HAVE HIM RUN THROUGH IT AGAIN!
IT'S GOOD FOR A GIRL'S MORALE!
...BUT HOW? HE CONSIDERS IT IDIOTIC!
3

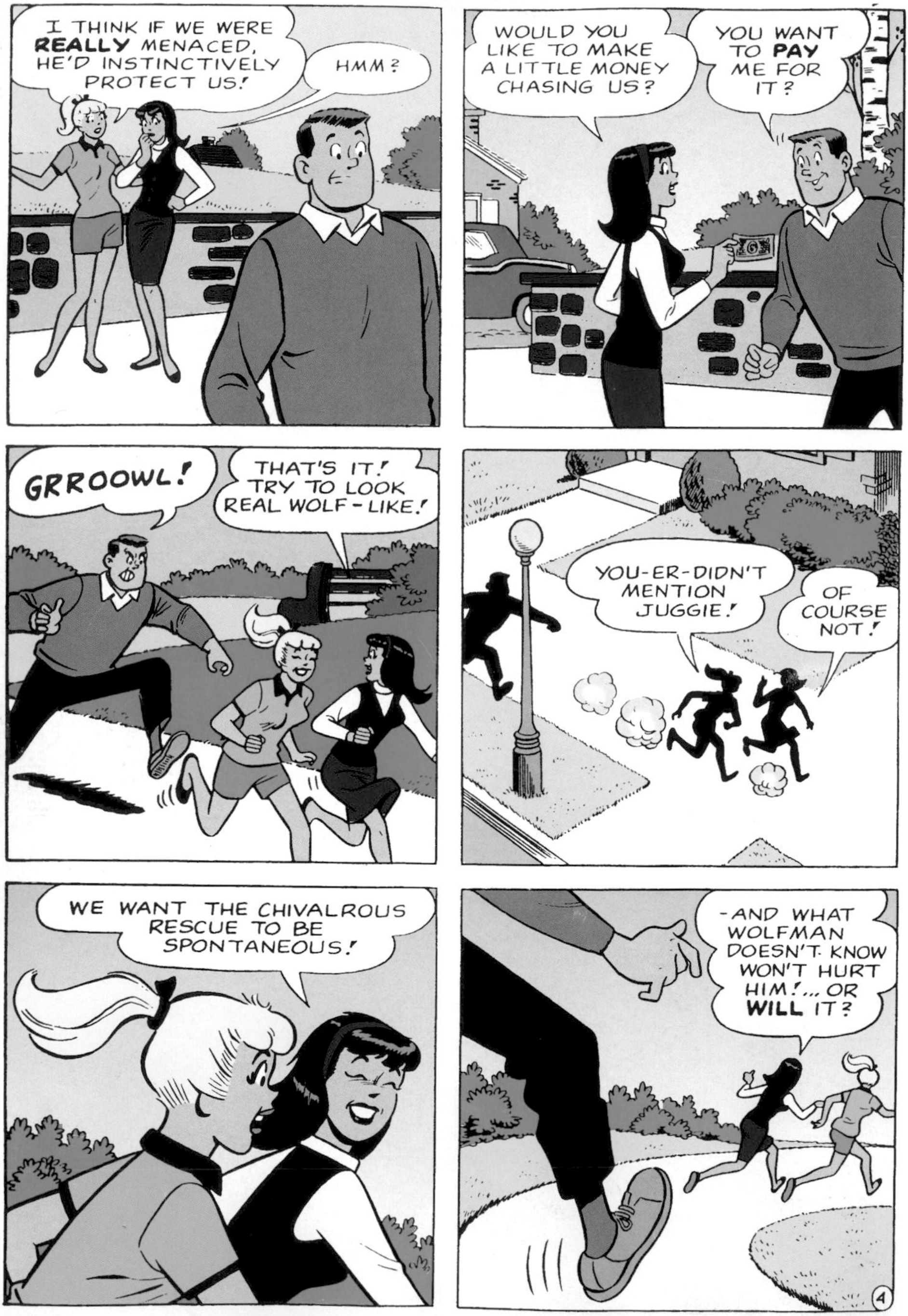
I THINK IF WE WERE **REALLY** MENACED, HE'D INSTINCTIVELY PROTECT US!
HMM?
WOULD YOU LIKE TO MAKE A LITTLE MONEY CHASING US?
YOU WANT TO **PAY** ME FOR IT?
GRROOWL!
THAT'S IT! TRY TO LOOK REAL WOLF-LIKE!
YOU-ER-DIDN'T MENTION JUGGIE!
OF COURSE NOT!
WE WANT THE CHIVALROUS RESCUE TO BE SPONTANEOUS!
-AND WHAT WOLFMAN DOESN'T KNOW WON'T HURT HIM!... OR **WILL** IT?
4

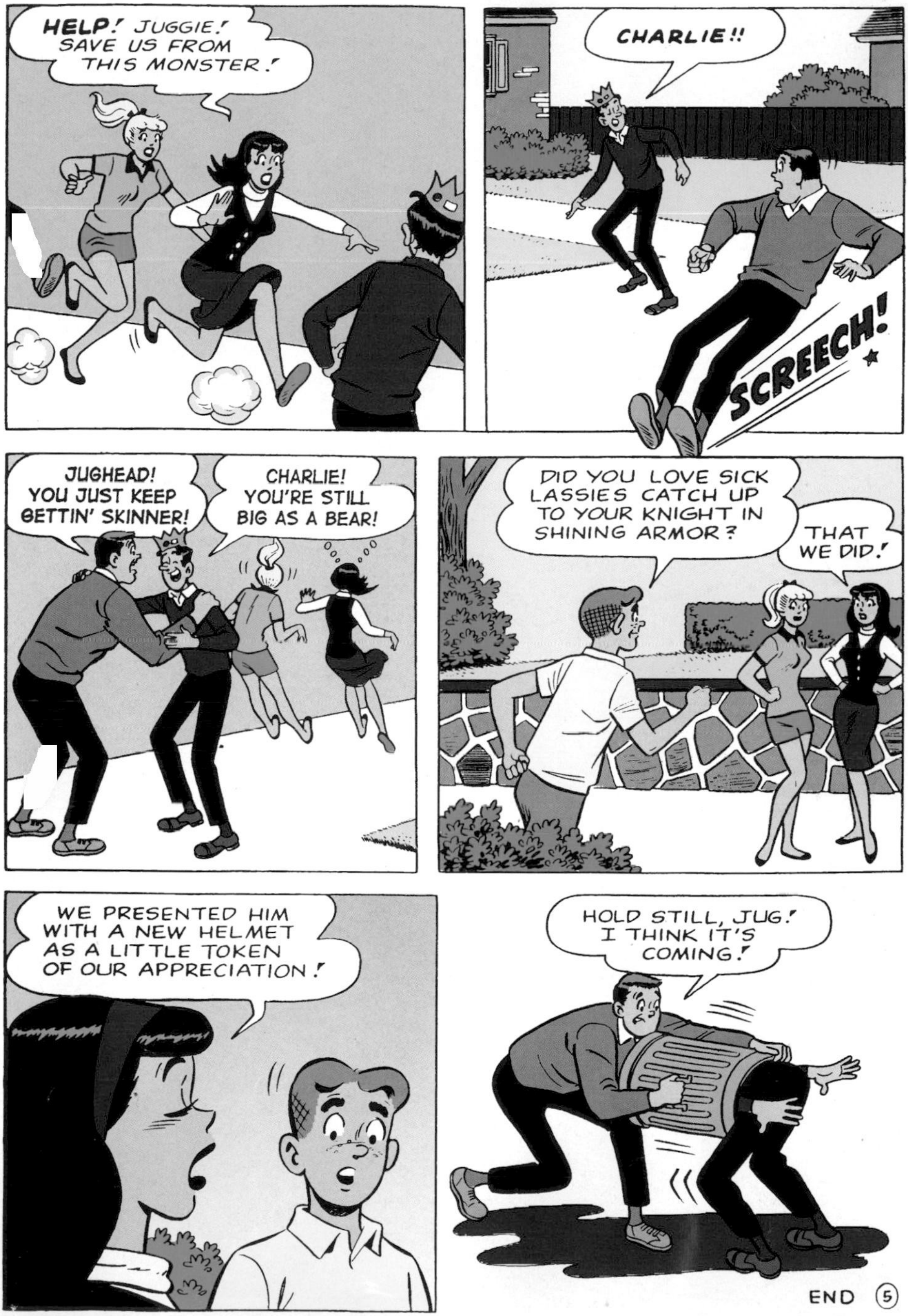
HELP! JUGGIE! SAVE US FROM THIS MONSTER!
CHARLIE!!
SCREECH!
JUGHEAD! YOU JUST KEEP GETTIN' SKINNER!
CHARLIE! YOU'RE STILL BIG AS A BEAR!
DID YOU LOVE SICK LASSIES CATCH UP TO YOUR KNIGHT IN SHINING ARMOR?
THAT WE DID!
WE PRESENTED HIM WITH A NEW HELMET AS A LITTLE TOKEN OF OUR APPRECIATION!
HOLD STILL, JUG! I THINK IT'S COMING!
END 5

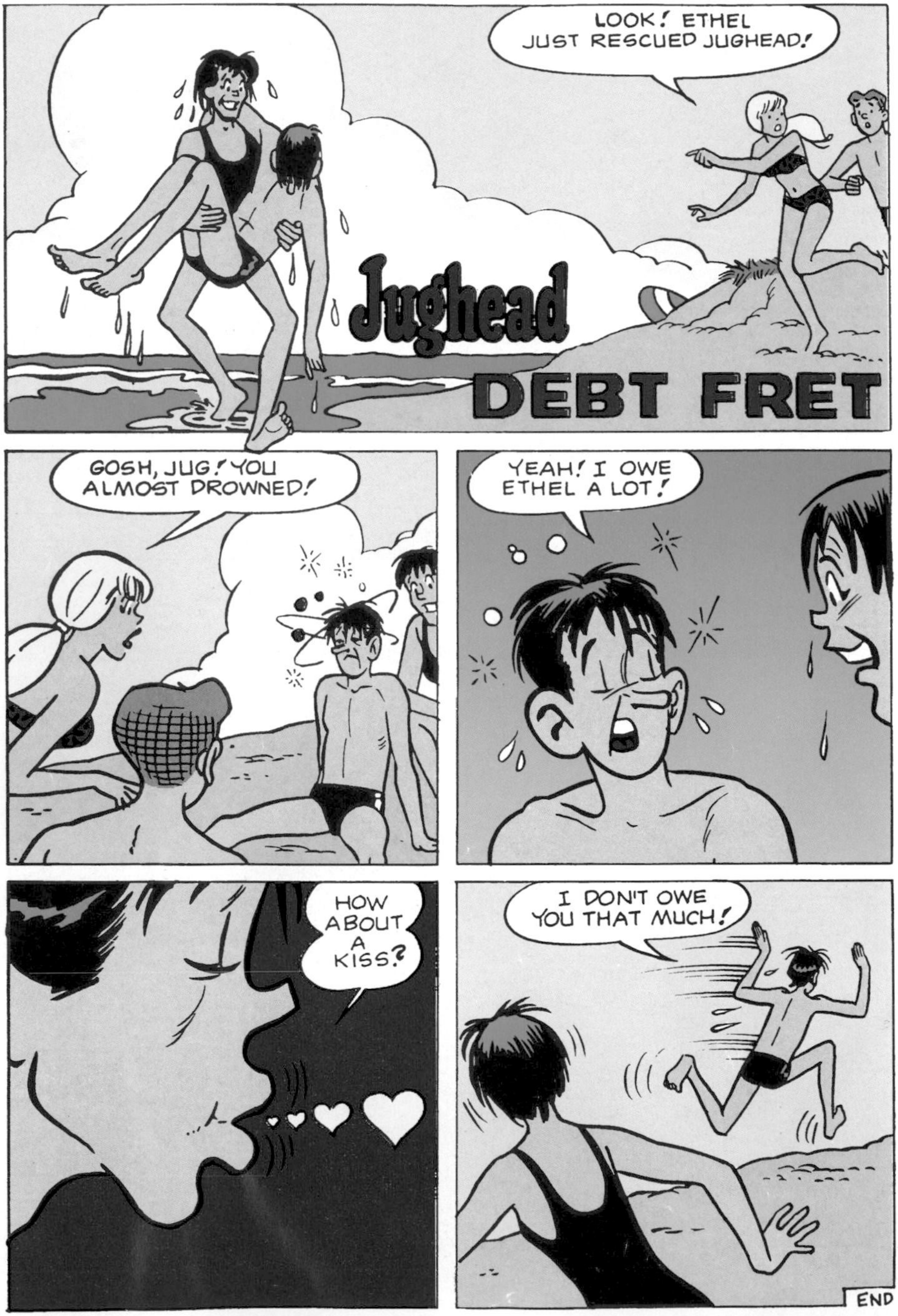
Jughead
DEBT FRET
LOOK! ETHEL JUST RESCUED JUGHEAD!
GOSH, JUG! YOU ALMOST DROWNED!
YEAH! I OWE ETHEL A LOT!
HOW ABOUT A KISS?
I DON'T OWE YOU THAT MUCH!
END

Archie & Friends in Au Revoir, Veronica

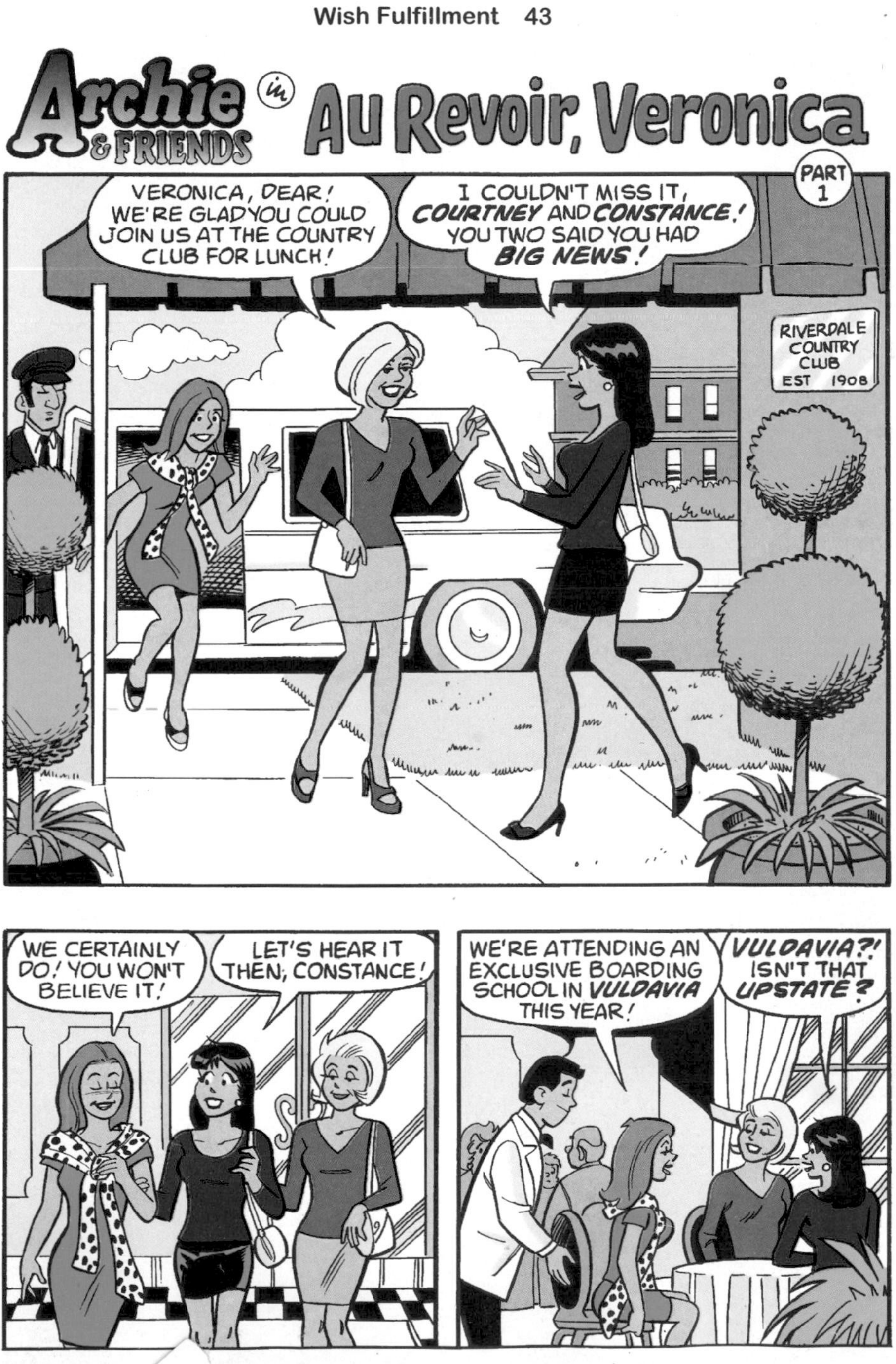
PART 1
VERONICA, DEAR! WE'RE GLAD YOU COULD JOIN US AT THE COUNTRY CLUB FOR LUNCH!
I COULDN'T MISS IT, COURTNEY AND CONSTANCE! YOU TWO SAID YOU HAD BIG NEWS!
RIVERDALE COUNTRY CLUB EST 1908
WE CERTAINLY DO! YOU WON'T BELIEVE IT!
LET'S HEAR IT THEN, CONSTANCE!
WE'RE ATTENDING AN EXCLUSIVE BOARDING SCHOOL IN VULDAVIA THIS YEAR!
VULDAVIA?! ISN'T THAT UPSTATE?

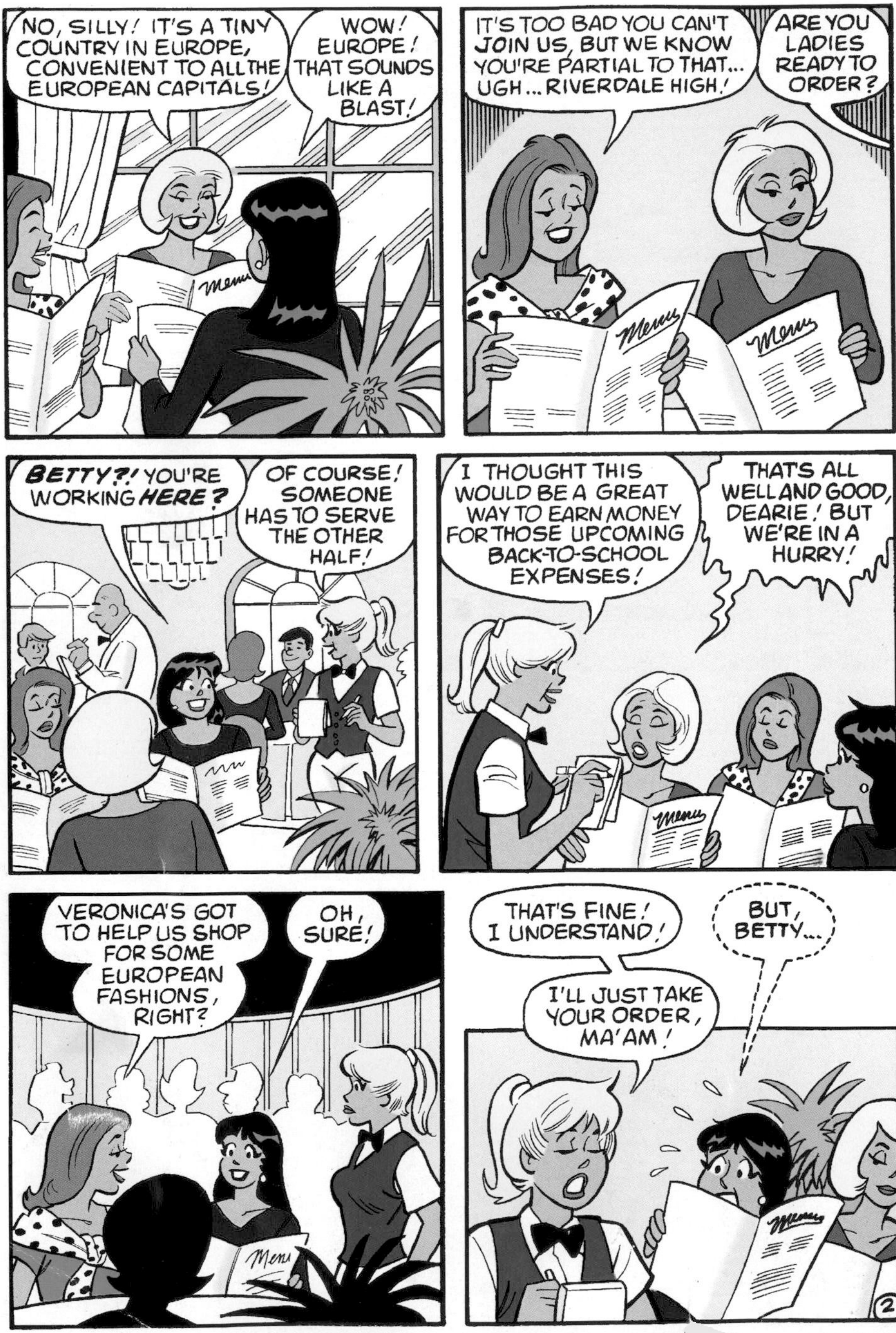
NO, SILLY! IT'S A TINY COUNTRY IN EUROPE, CONVENIENT TO ALL THE EUROPEAN CAPITALS!
WOW! EUROPE! THAT SOUNDS LIKE A BLAST!
Menu
IT'S TOO BAD YOU CAN'T JOIN US, BUT WE KNOW YOU'RE PARTIAL TO THAT... UGH... RIVERDALE HIGH!
ARE YOU LADIES READY TO ORDER?
Menu
Menu
BETTY?! YOU'RE WORKING HERE?
OF COURSE! SOMEONE HAS TO SERVE THE OTHER HALF!
I THOUGHT THIS WOULD BE A GREAT WAY TO EARN MONEY FOR THOSE UPCOMING BACK-TO-SCHOOL EXPENSES!
THAT'S ALL WELL AND GOOD, DEARIE! BUT WE'RE IN A HURRY!
Menu
VERONICA'S GOT TO HELP US SHOP FOR SOME EUROPEAN FASHIONS, RIGHT?
OH, SURE!
Menu
THAT'S FINE! I UNDERSTAND!
BUT, BETTY...
I'LL JUST TAKE YOUR ORDER, MA'AM!
Menu
2

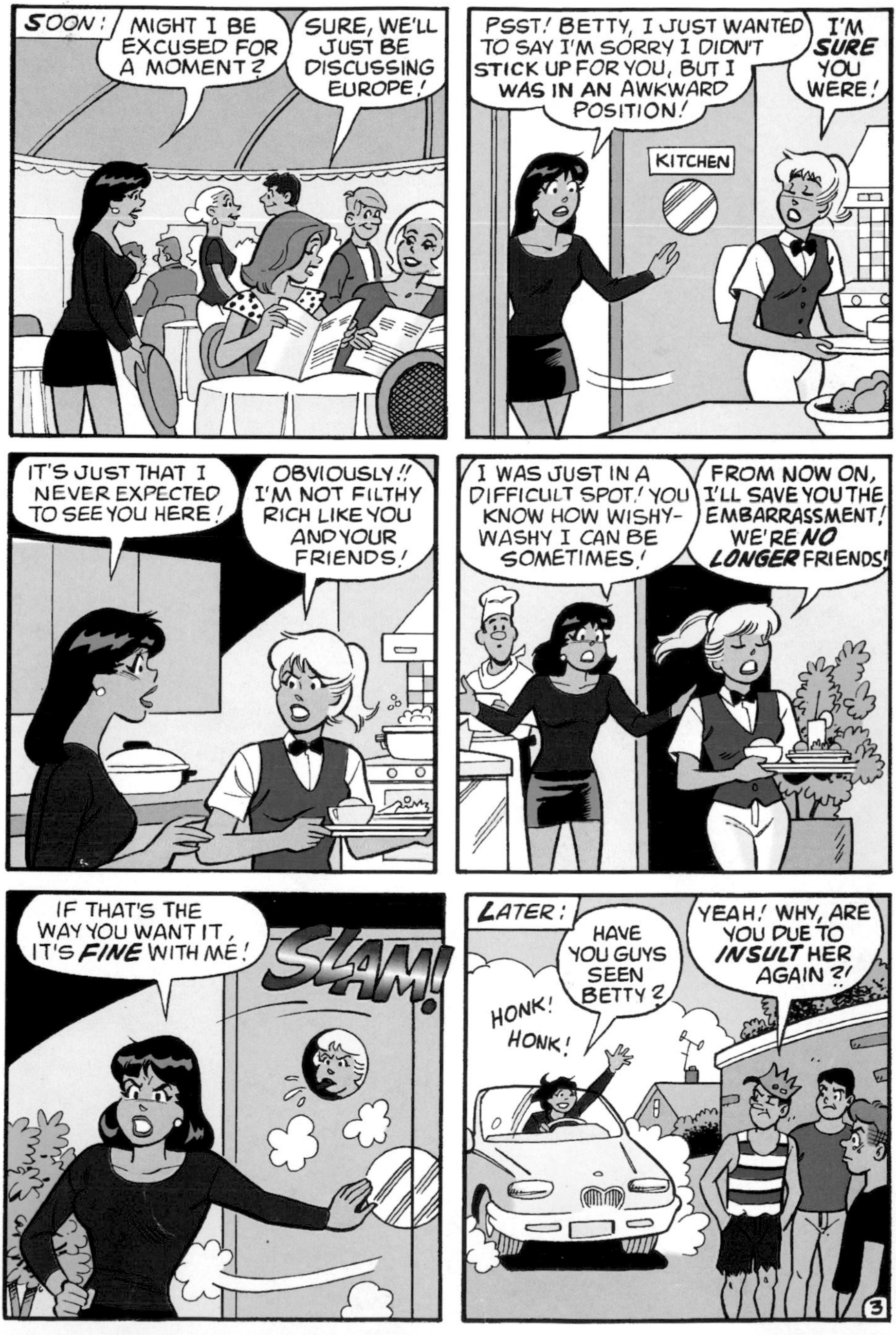
SOON:
MIGHT I BE EXCUSED FOR A MOMENT?
SURE, WE'LL JUST BE DISCUSSING EUROPE!
PSST! BETTY, I JUST WANTED TO SAY I'M SORRY I DIDN'T STICK UP FOR YOU, BUT I WAS IN AN AWKWARD POSITION!
I'M SURE YOU WERE!
KITCHEN
IT'S JUST THAT I NEVER EXPECTED TO SEE YOU HERE!
OBVIOUSLY!! I'M NOT FILTHY RICH LIKE YOU AND YOUR FRIENDS!
I WAS JUST IN A DIFFICULT SPOT! YOU KNOW HOW WISHY-WASHY I CAN BE SOMETIMES!
FROM NOW ON, I'LL SAVE YOU THE EMBARRASSMENT! WE'RE NO LONGER FRIENDS!
IF THAT'S THE WAY YOU WANT IT, IT'S FINE WITH ME!
SLAM!
LATER:
HAVE YOU GUYS SEEN BETTY?
HONK! HONK!
YEAH! WHY, ARE YOU DUE TO INSULT HER AGAIN?!
3

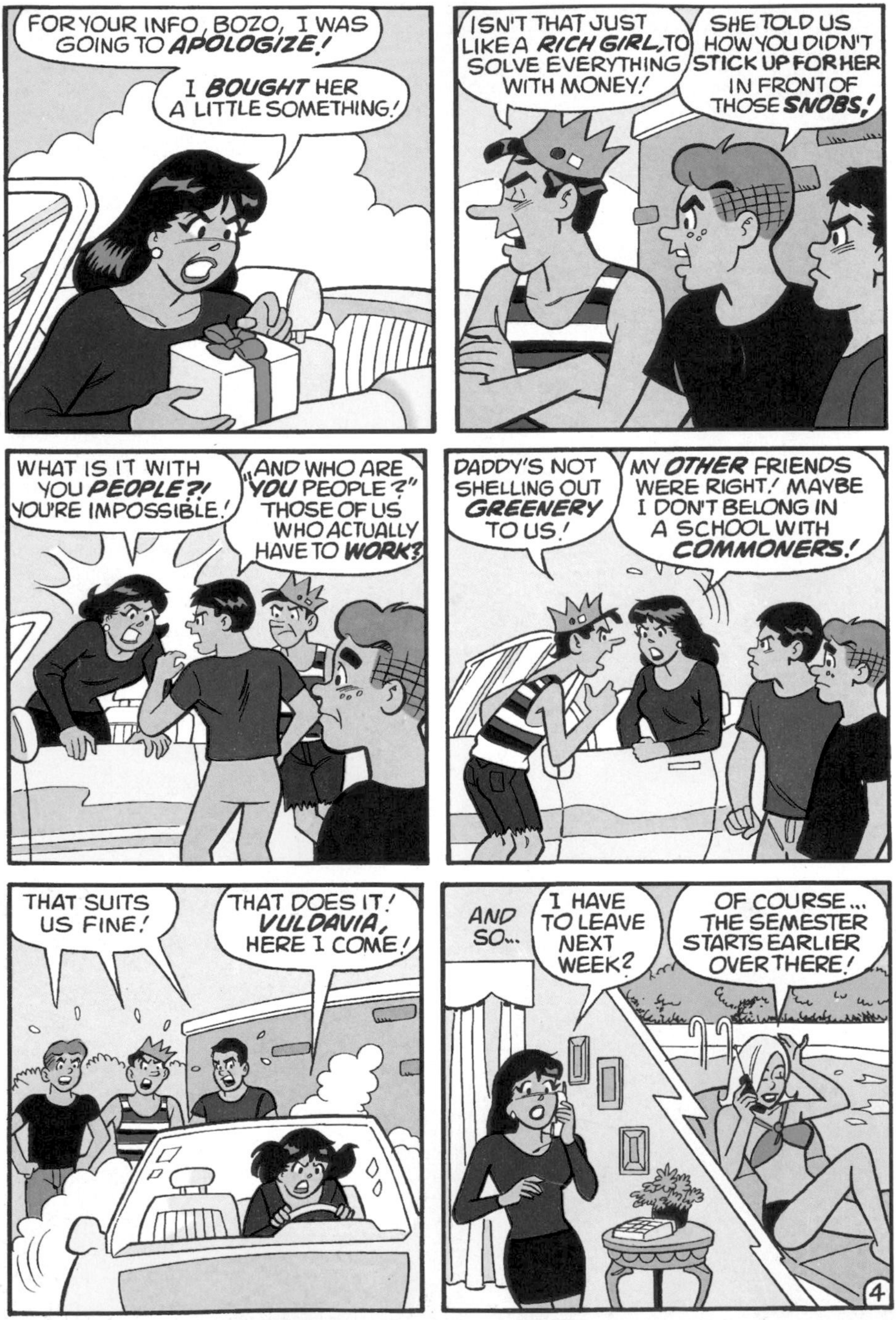
FOR YOUR INFO, BOZO, I WAS GOING TO APOLOGIZE!
I BOUGHT HER A LITTLE SOMETHING!
ISN'T THAT JUST LIKE A RICH GIRL, TO SOLVE EVERYTHING WITH MONEY!
SHE TOLD US HOW YOU DIDN'T STICK UP FOR HER IN FRONT OF THOSE SNOBS!
WHAT IS IT WITH YOU PEOPLE?! YOU'RE IMPOSSIBLE!
"AND WHO ARE YOU PEOPLE?" THOSE OF US WHO ACTUALLY HAVE TO WORK?
DADDY'S NOT SHELLING OUT GREENERY TO US!
MY OTHER FRIENDS WERE RIGHT! MAYBE I DON'T BELONG IN A SCHOOL WITH COMMONERS!
THAT SUITS US FINE!
THAT DOES IT! VULDAVIA, HERE I COME!
AND SO...
I HAVE TO LEAVE NEXT WEEK?
OF COURSE... THE SEMESTER STARTS EARLIER OVER THERE!
4

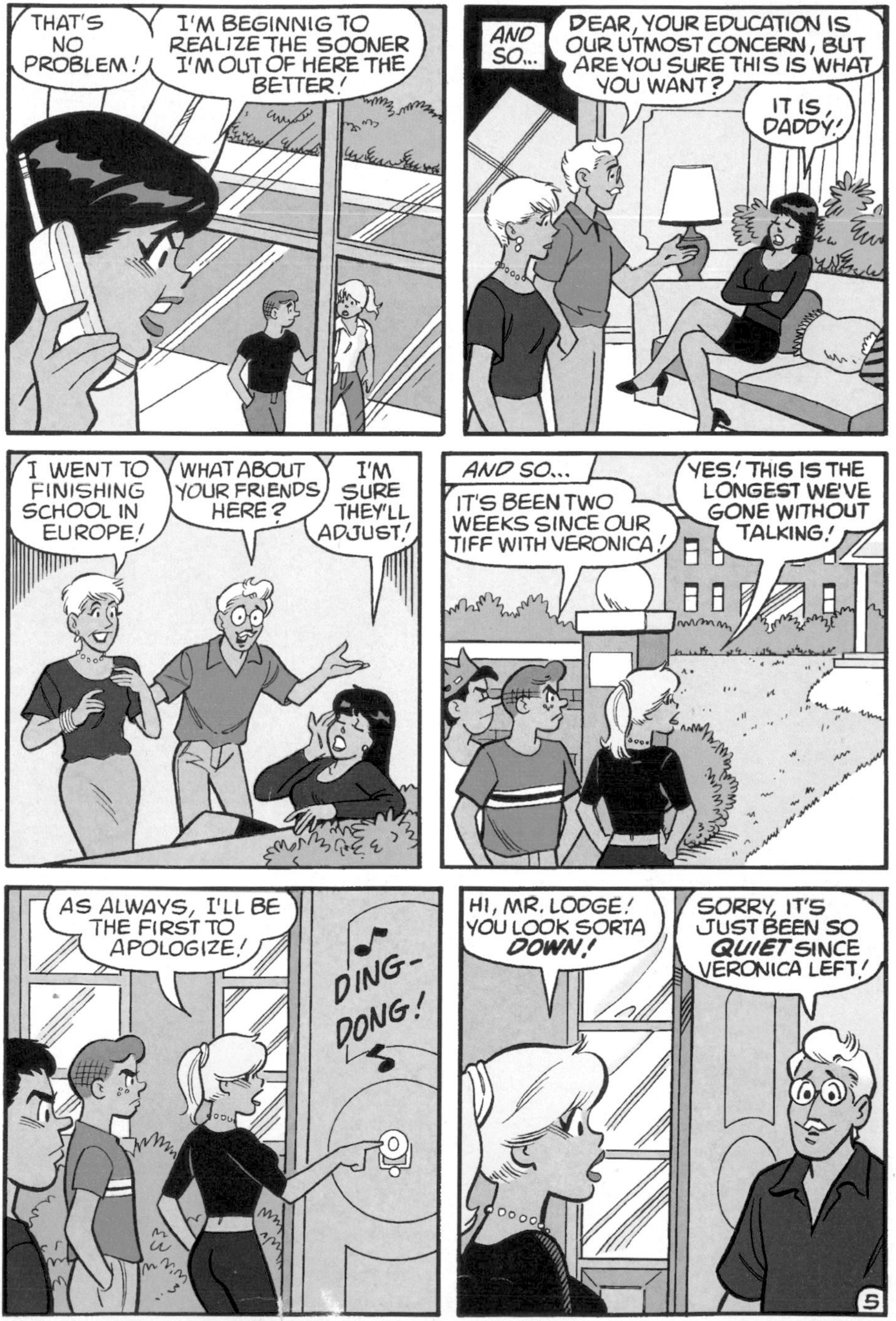
THAT'S NO PROBLEM!
I'M BEGINNIG TO REALIZE THE SOONER I'M OUT OF HERE THE BETTER!
AND SO...
DEAR, YOUR EDUCATION IS OUR UTMOST CONCERN, BUT ARE YOU SURE THIS IS WHAT YOU WANT?
IT IS, DADDY!
I WENT TO FINISHING SCHOOL IN EUROPE!
WHAT ABOUT YOUR FRIENDS HERE?
I'M SURE THEY'LL ADJUST!
AND SO...
IT'S BEEN TWO WEEKS SINCE OUR TIFF WITH VERONICA!
YES! THIS IS THE LONGEST WE'VE GONE WITHOUT TALKING!
AS ALWAYS, I'LL BE THE FIRST TO APOLOGIZE!
DING-DONG!
HI, MR. LODGE! YOU LOOK SORTA DOWN!
SORRY, IT'S JUST BEEN SO QUIET SINCE VERONICA LEFT!
5

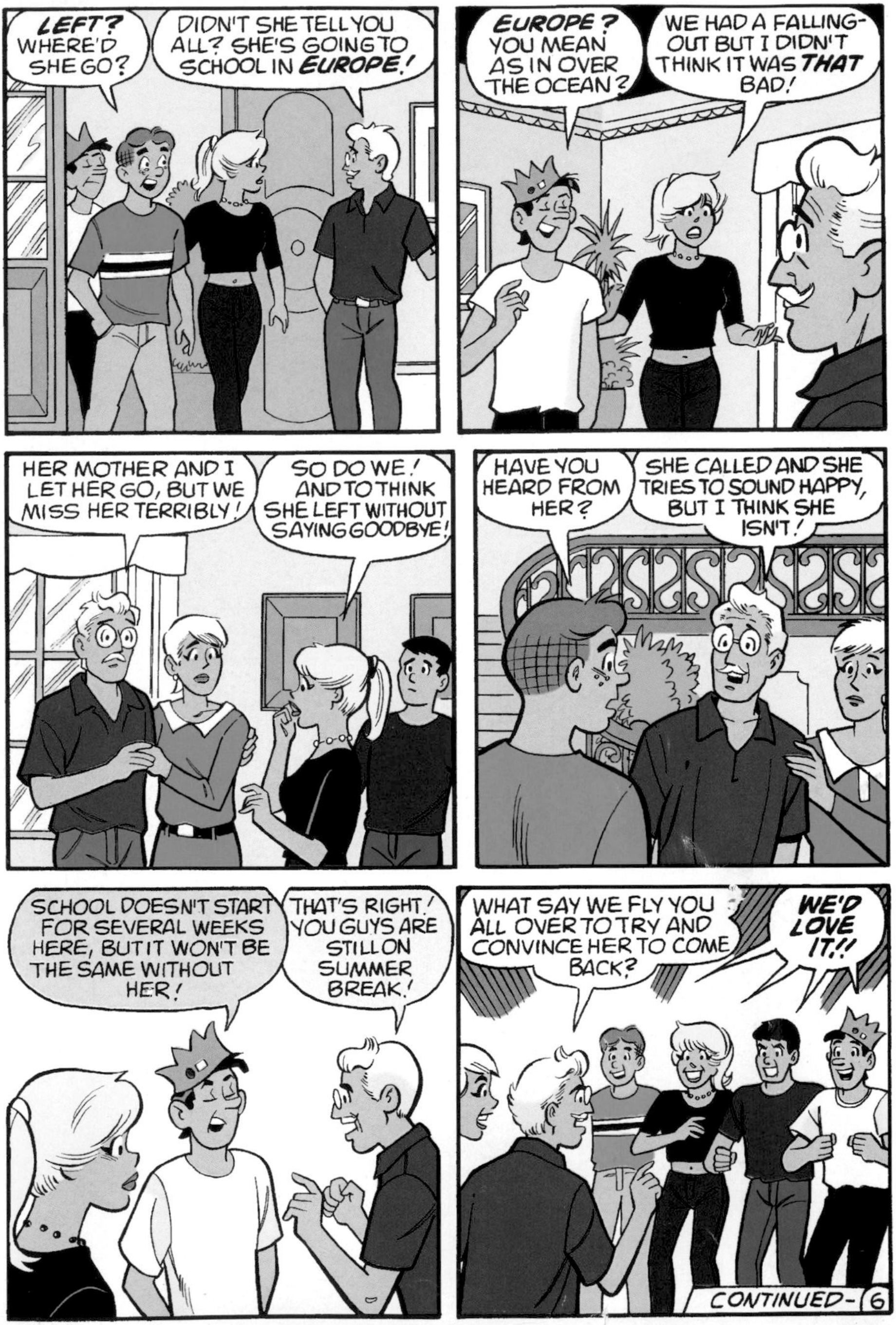
LEFT? WHERE'D SHE GO?
DIDN'T SHE TELL YOU ALL? SHE'S GOING TO SCHOOL IN EUROPE!
EUROPE? YOU MEAN AS IN OVER THE OCEAN?
WE HAD A FALLING-OUT BUT I DIDN'T THINK IT WAS THAT BAD!
HER MOTHER AND I LET HER GO, BUT WE MISS HER TERRIBLY!
SO DO WE! AND TO THINK SHE LEFT WITHOUT SAYING GOODBYE!
HAVE YOU HEARD FROM HER?
SHE CALLED AND SHE TRIES TO SOUND HAPPY, BUT I THINK SHE ISN'T!
SCHOOL DOESN'T START FOR SEVERAL WEEKS HERE, BUT IT WON'T BE THE SAME WITHOUT HER!
THAT'S RIGHT! YOU GUYS ARE STILL ON SUMMER BREAK!
WHAT SAY WE FLY YOU ALL OVER TO TRY AND CONVINCE HER TO COME BACK?
WE'D LOVE IT!!
CONTINUED- 6

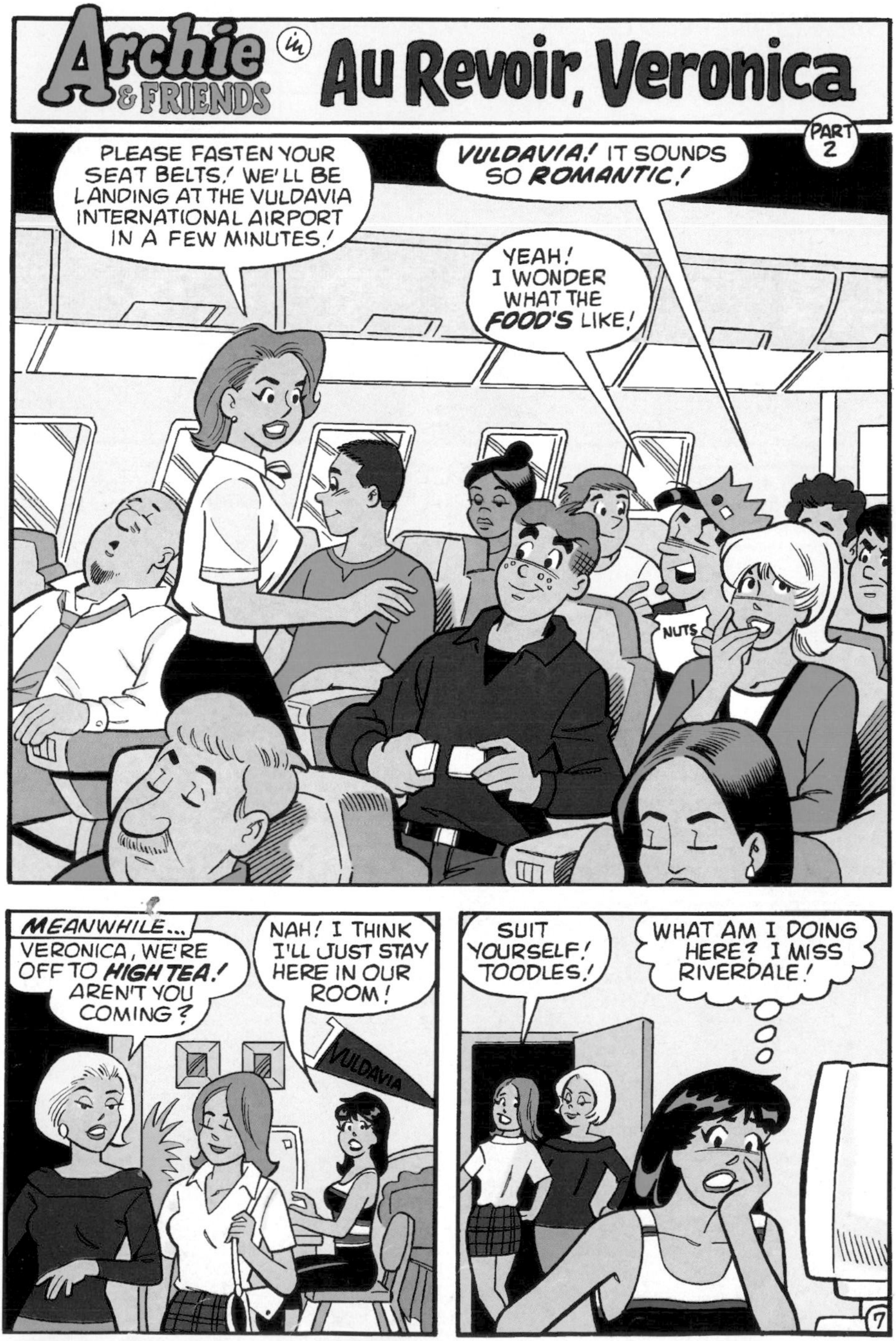
Archie & FRIENDS in
Au Revoir, Veronica
PART 2
PLEASE FASTEN YOUR SEAT BELTS! WE'LL BE LANDING AT THE VULDAVIA INTERNATIONAL AIRPORT IN A FEW MINUTES!
VULDAVIA! IT SOUNDS SO ROMANTIC!
YEAH! I WONDER WHAT THE FOOD'S LIKE!
NUTS
MEANWHILE...
VERONICA, WE'RE OFF TO HIGH TEA! AREN'T YOU COMING?
NAH! I THINK I'LL JUST STAY HERE IN OUR ROOM!
VULDAVIA
SUIT YOURSELF! TOODLES!
WHAT AM I DOING HERE? I MISS RIVERDALE!
7

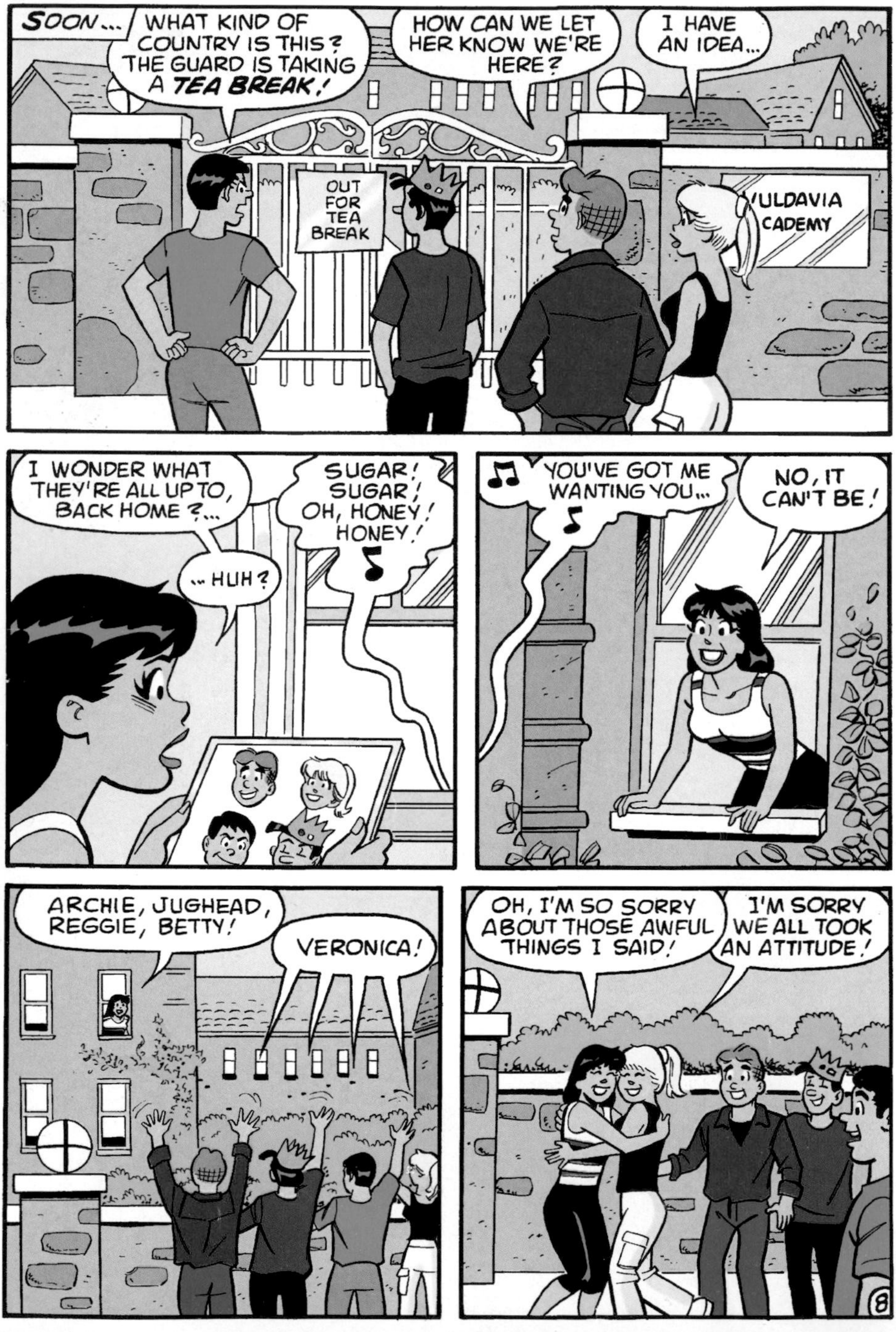
SOON...
WHAT KIND OF COUNTRY IS THIS? THE GUARD IS TAKING A TEA BREAK!
HOW CAN WE LET HER KNOW WE'RE HERE?
I HAVE AN IDEA...
OUT FOR TEA BREAK
VULDAVIA CADEMY
I WONDER WHAT THEY'RE ALL UP TO, BACK HOME?...
SUGAR! SUGAR! OH, HONEY! HONEY!
...HUH?
YOU'VE GOT ME WANTING YOU...
NO, IT CAN'T BE!
ARCHIE, JUGHEAD, REGGIE, BETTY!
VERONICA!
OH, I'M SO SORRY ABOUT THOSE AWFUL THINGS I SAID!
I'M SORRY WE ALL TOOK AN ATTITUDE!
8

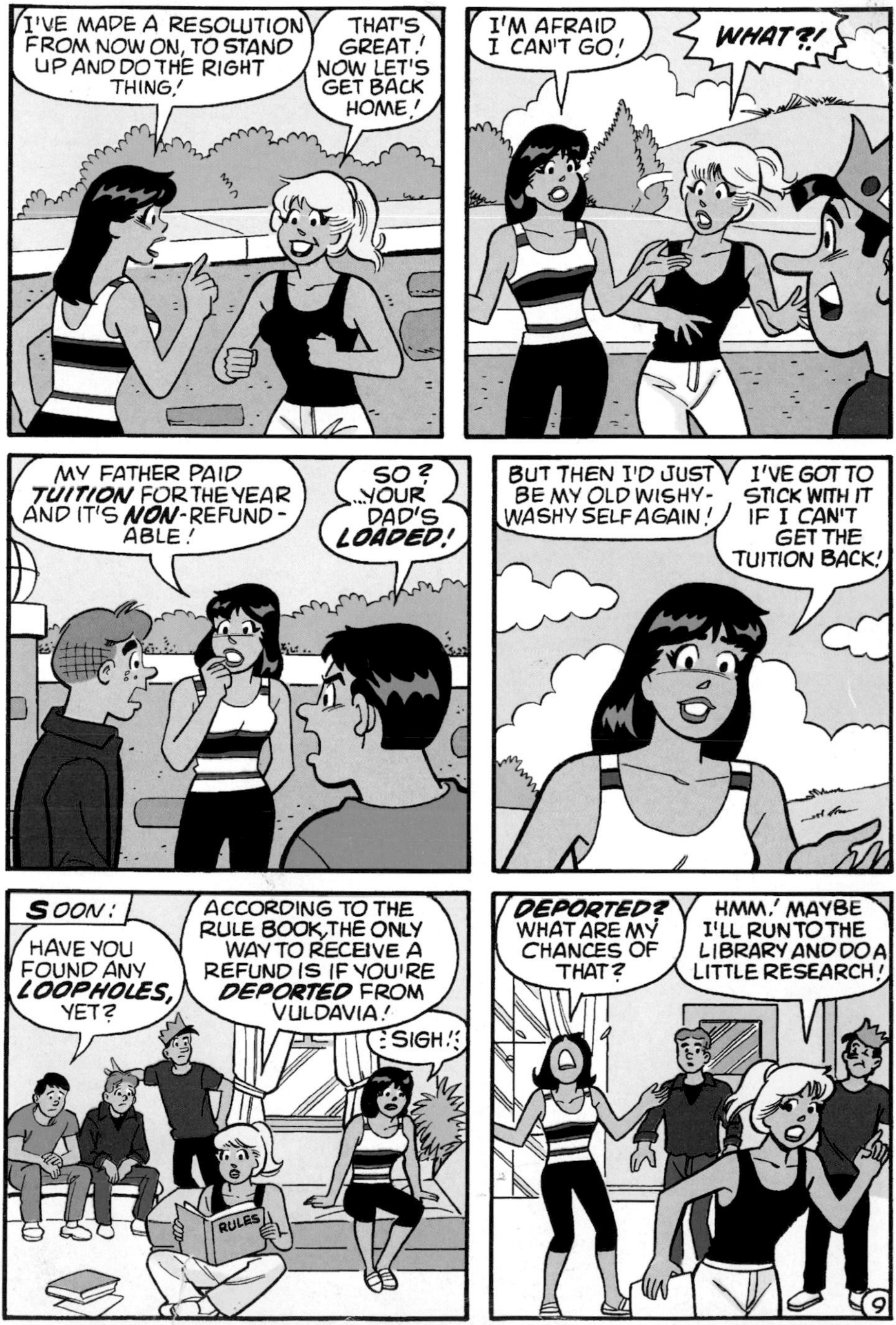
I'VE MADE A RESOLUTION FROM NOW ON, TO STAND UP AND DO THE RIGHT THING!
THAT'S GREAT! NOW LET'S GET BACK HOME!
I'M AFRAID I CAN'T GO!
WHAT?!
MY FATHER PAID TUITION FOR THE YEAR AND IT'S NON-REFUNDABLE!
SO? ...YOUR DAD'S LOADED!
BUT THEN I'D JUST BE MY OLD WISHY-WASHY SELF AGAIN!
I'VE GOT TO STICK WITH IT IF I CAN'T GET THE TUITION BACK!
SOON:
HAVE YOU FOUND ANY LOOPHOLES, YET?
ACCORDING TO THE RULE BOOK, THE ONLY WAY TO RECEIVE A REFUND IS IF YOU'RE DEPORTED FROM VULDAVIA!
SIGH!
RULES
DEPORTED? WHAT ARE MY CHANCES OF THAT?
HMM! MAYBE I'LL RUN TO THE LIBRARY AND DO A LITTLE RESEARCH!
9

LATER:

TWEET!

SHE MUST'VE FOUND SOMETHING! WE'RE ON OUR WAY DOWN!

TAKE THESE!

WHAT?

PROTEST SIGNS!

VULDAVIA IS A BORE!

VULDAVIA STINKS!

VULDAVIA IS VULG...

HOW'S A LITTLE PROTESTING GOING TO GET MY MONEY BACK?

RRRRR

VULDAVIA IS A BORE!

LDAVIA IS BOR-ING

VULDAVIA STINKS!

VUL... IS VULG...

OKAY, EVERYONE... IN THE WAGON!

WHAT FOR?

VULDAVIA POLICE

VULDAVIA STINKS!

VULDAVIA

VULD... IS A BOR...

YOU'RE ALL UNDER ARREST!

ARREST?!

VULDAVIA STINKS!

I FOUND OUT AT THE LIBRARY IT'S ILLEGAL TO PROTEST IN VULDAVIA!

OF COURSE, ALL CITIZENS KNOW THAT!

VULDAVIA IS...

VULDAVIA STINKS!

10

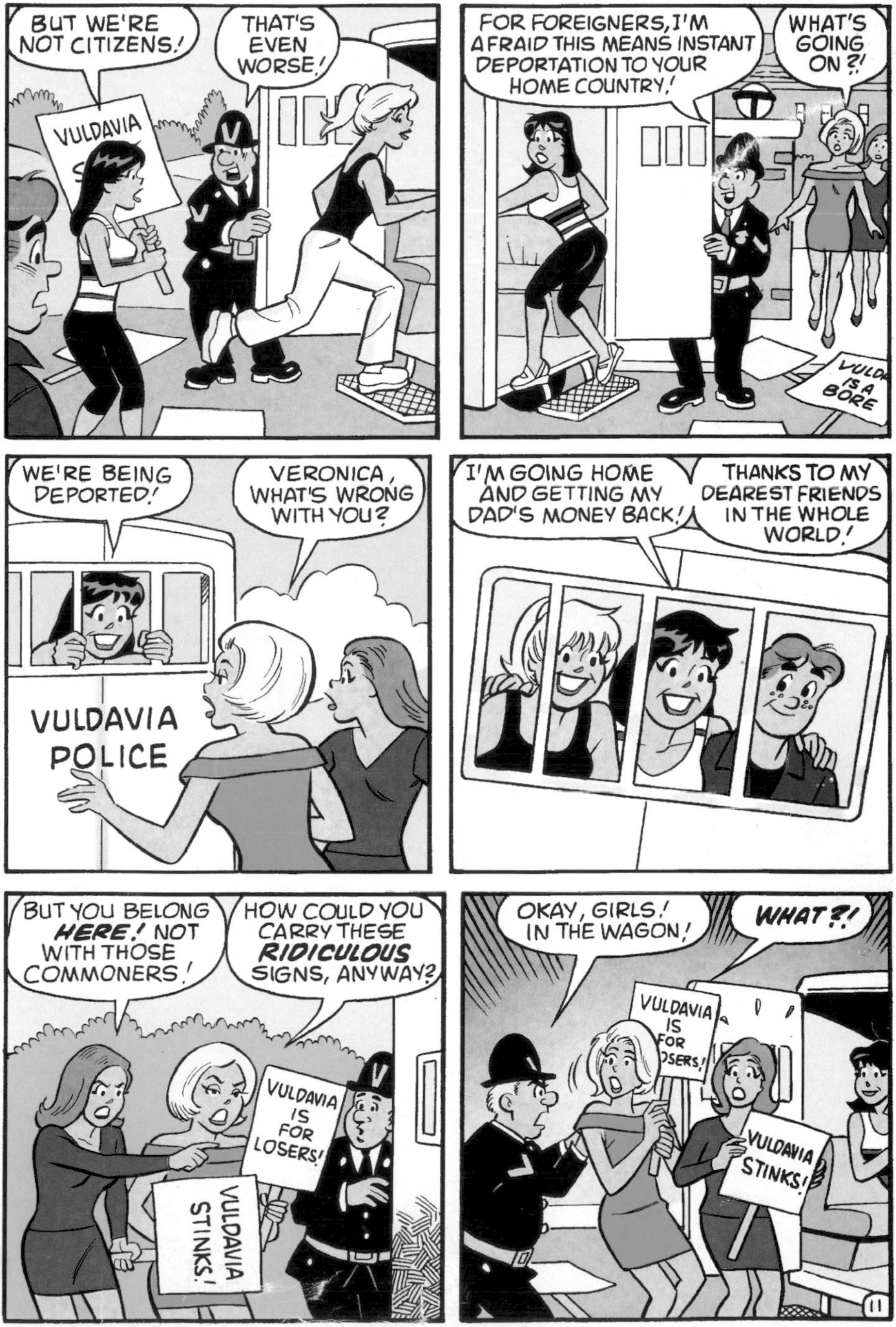
BUT WE'RE NOT CITIZENS!
VULDAVIA
THAT'S EVEN WORSE!
FOR FOREIGNERS, I'M AFRAID THIS MEANS INSTANT DEPORTATION TO YOUR HOME COUNTRY!
WHAT'S GOING ON?!
VULDA IS A BORE
WE'RE BEING DEPORTED!
VERONICA, WHAT'S WRONG WITH YOU?
VULDAVIA POLICE
I'M GOING HOME AND GETTING MY DAD'S MONEY BACK!
THANKS TO MY DEAREST FRIENDS IN THE WHOLE WORLD!
BUT YOU BELONG HERE! NOT WITH THOSE COMMONERS!
HOW COULD YOU CARRY THESE RIDICULOUS SIGNS, ANYWAY?
VULDAVIA IS FOR LOSERS!
VULDAVIA STINKS!
OKAY, GIRLS! IN THE WAGON!
WHAT?!
VULDAVIA IS FOR LOSERS!
VULDAVIA STINKS!
11

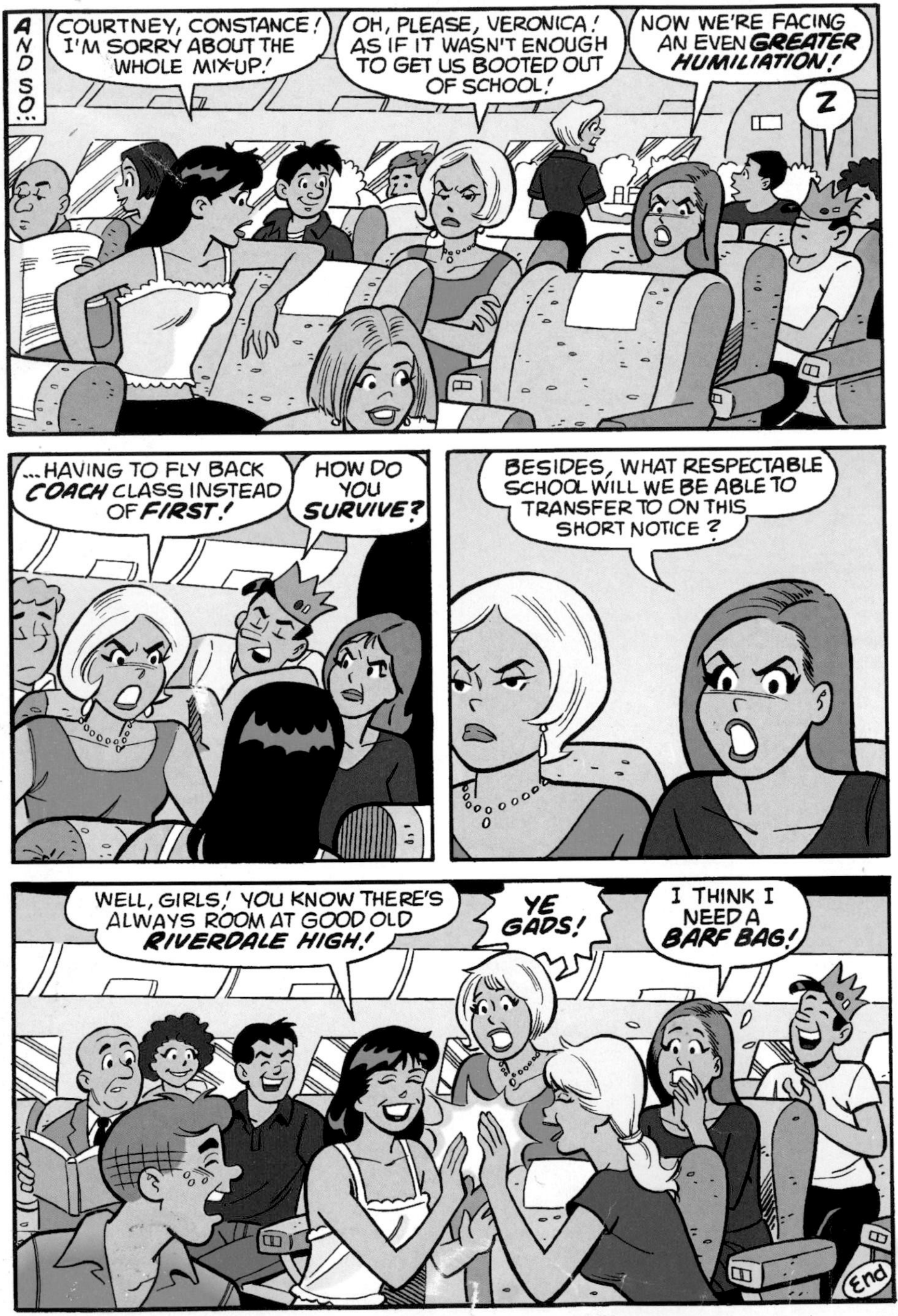
AND SO...
COURTNEY, CONSTANCE! I'M SORRY ABOUT THE WHOLE MIX-UP!
OH, PLEASE, VERONICA! AS IF IT WASN'T ENOUGH TO GET US BOOTED OUT OF SCHOOL!
NOW WE'RE FACING AN EVEN GREATER HUMILIATION!
Z
...HAVING TO FLY BACK COACH CLASS INSTEAD OF FIRST!
HOW DO YOU SURVIVE?
BESIDES, WHAT RESPECTABLE SCHOOL WILL WE BE ABLE TO TRANSFER TO ON THIS SHORT NOTICE?
WELL, GIRLS! YOU KNOW THERE'S ALWAYS ROOM AT GOOD OLD RIVERDALE HIGH!
YE GADS!
I THINK I NEED A BARF BAG!
End

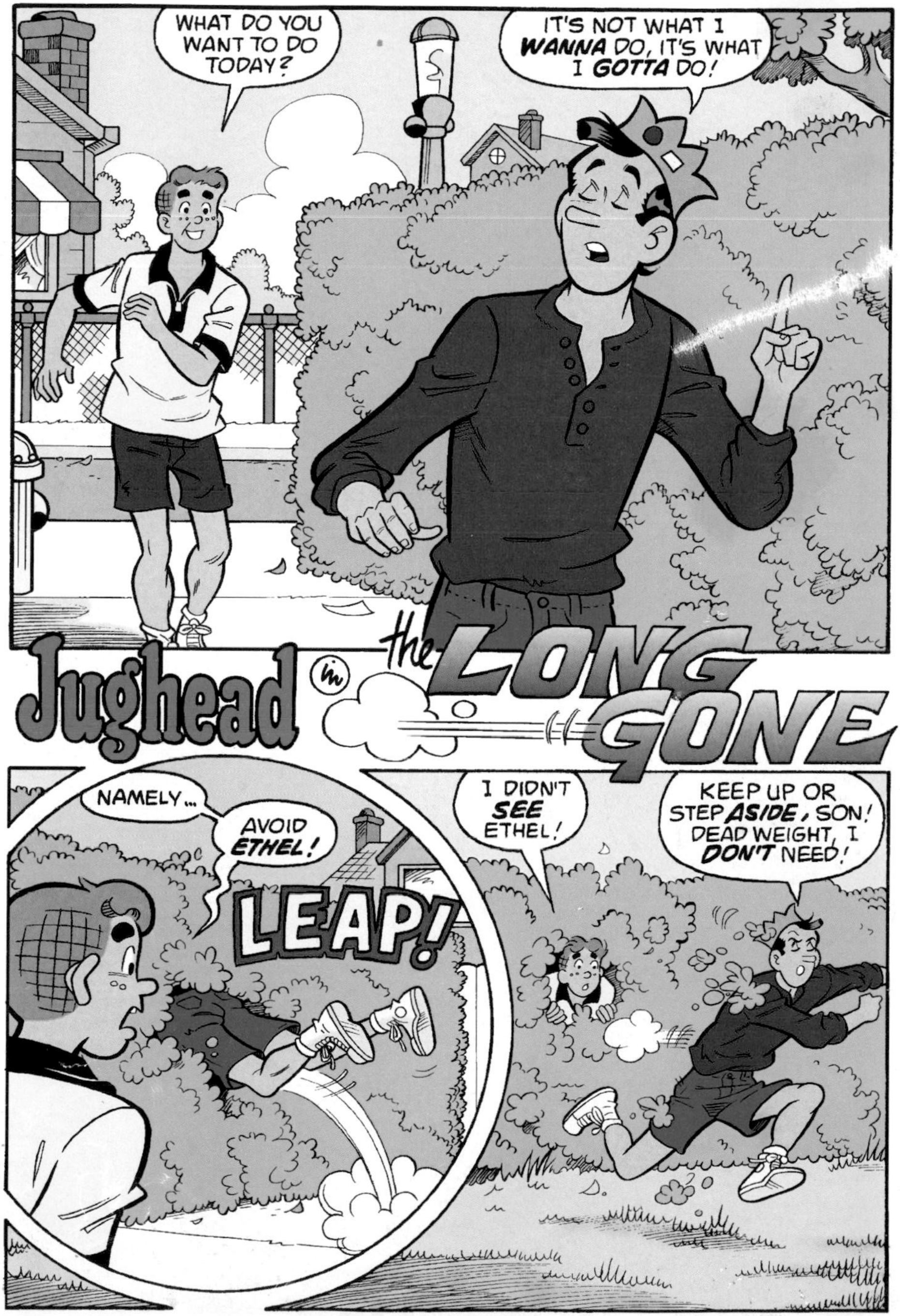
WHAT DO YOU WANT TO DO TODAY?
IT'S NOT WHAT I WANNA DO, IT'S WHAT I GOTTA DO!
Jughead in the LONG GONE
NAMELY...
AVOID ETHEL!
LEAP!
I DIDN'T SEE ETHEL!
KEEP UP OR STEP ASIDE, SON! DEAD WEIGHT, I DON'T NEED!

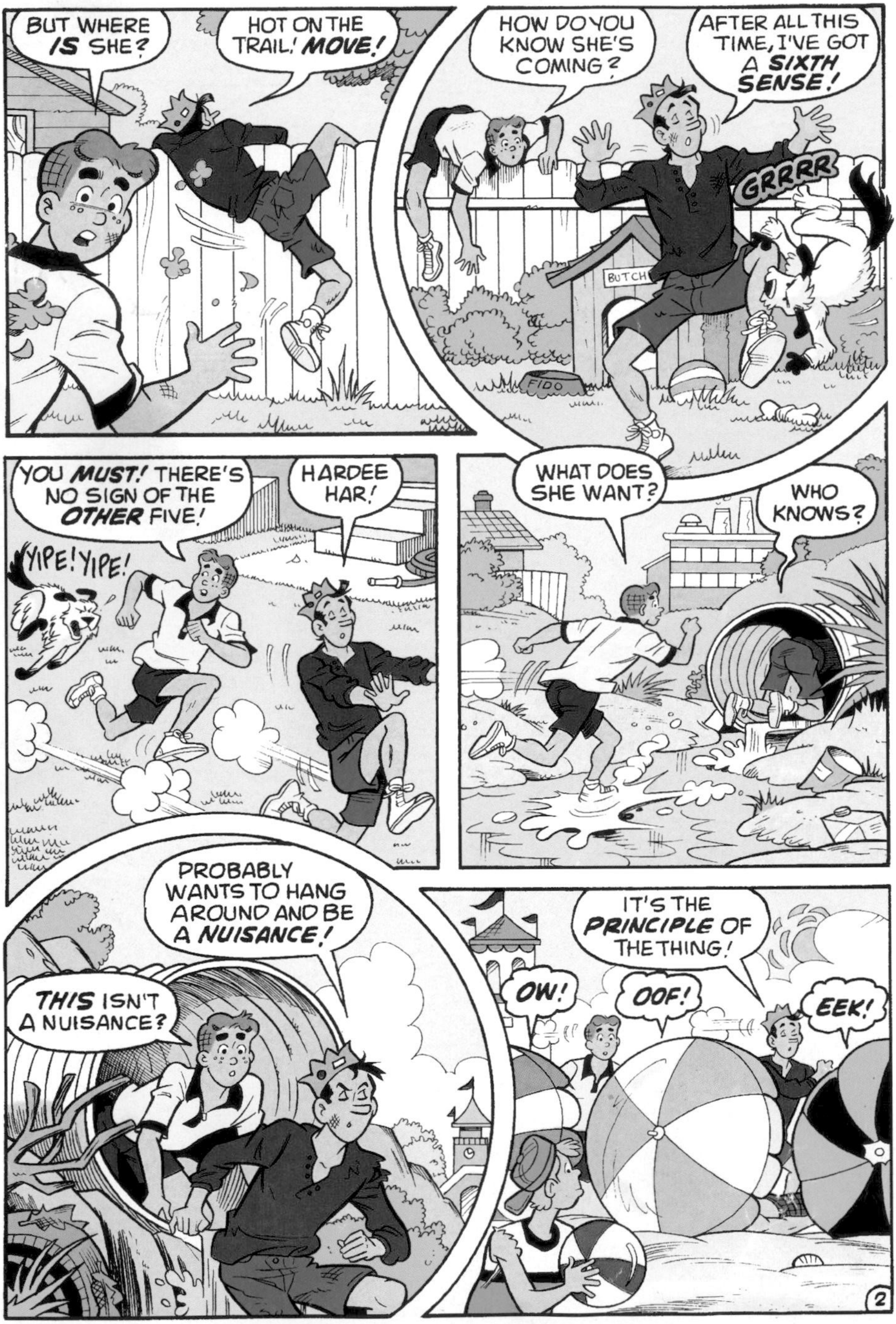
BUT WHERE *IS* SHE?
HOT ON THE TRAIL! *MOVE!*
HOW DO YOU KNOW SHE'S COMING?
AFTER ALL THIS TIME, I'VE GOT A *SIXTH SENSE!*
GRRRR
BUTCH
FIDO
YOU *MUST!* THERE'S NO SIGN OF THE *OTHER* FIVE!
HARDEE HAR!
YIPE! YIPE!
WHAT DOES SHE WANT?
WHO KNOWS?
PROBABLY WANTS TO HANG AROUND AND BE A *NUISANCE!*
THIS ISN'T A NUISANCE?
IT'S THE *PRINCIPLE* OF THE THING!
OW!
OOF!
EEK!
2

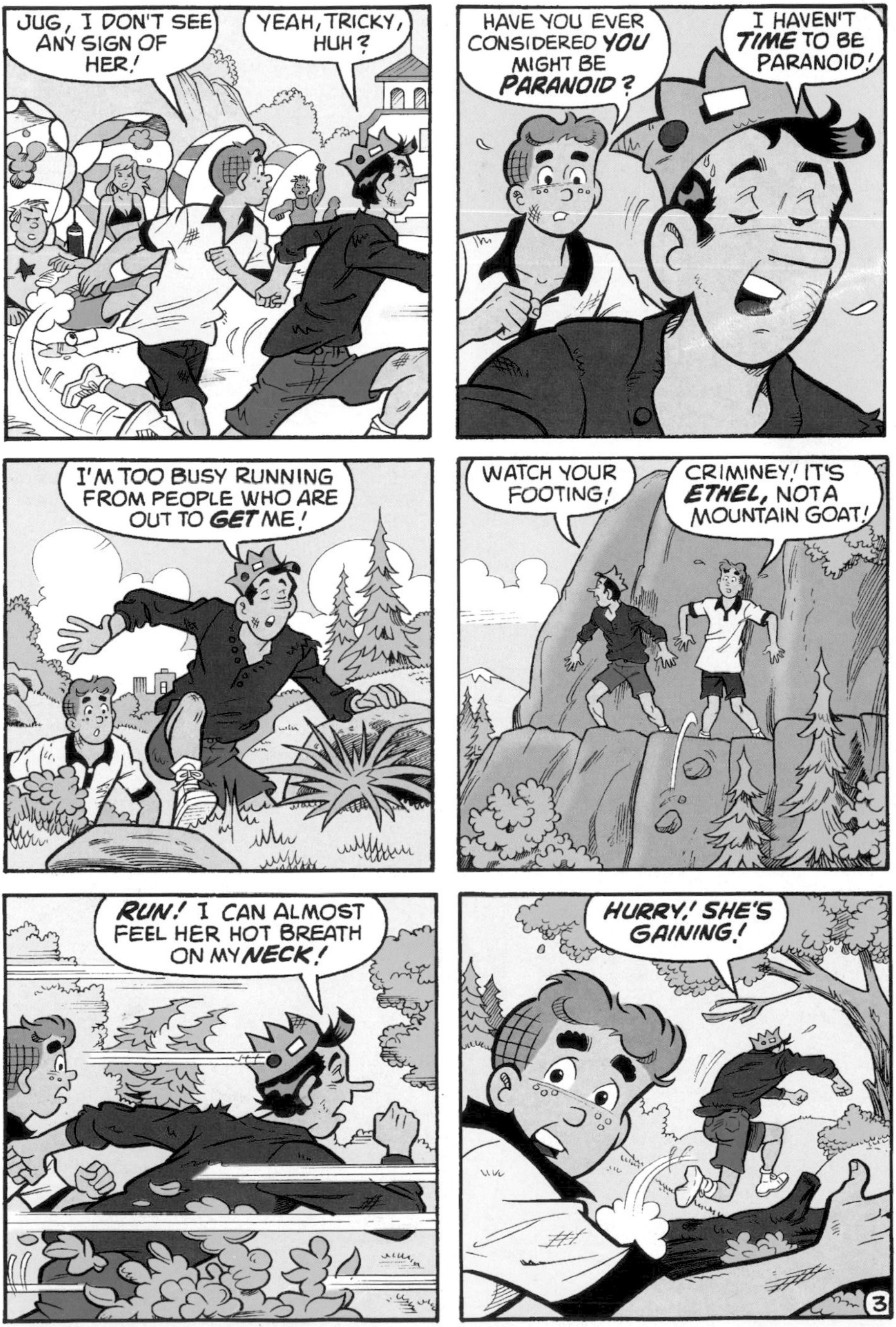
JUG, I DON'T SEE ANY SIGN OF HER!
YEAH, TRICKY, HUH?
HAVE YOU EVER CONSIDERED YOU MIGHT BE PARANOID?
I HAVEN'T TIME TO BE PARANOID!
I'M TOO BUSY RUNNING FROM PEOPLE WHO ARE OUT TO GET ME!
WATCH YOUR FOOTING!
CRIMINEY! IT'S ETHEL, NOT A MOUNTAIN GOAT!
RUN! I CAN ALMOST FEEL HER HOT BREATH ON MY NECK!
HURRY! SHE'S GAINING!
3

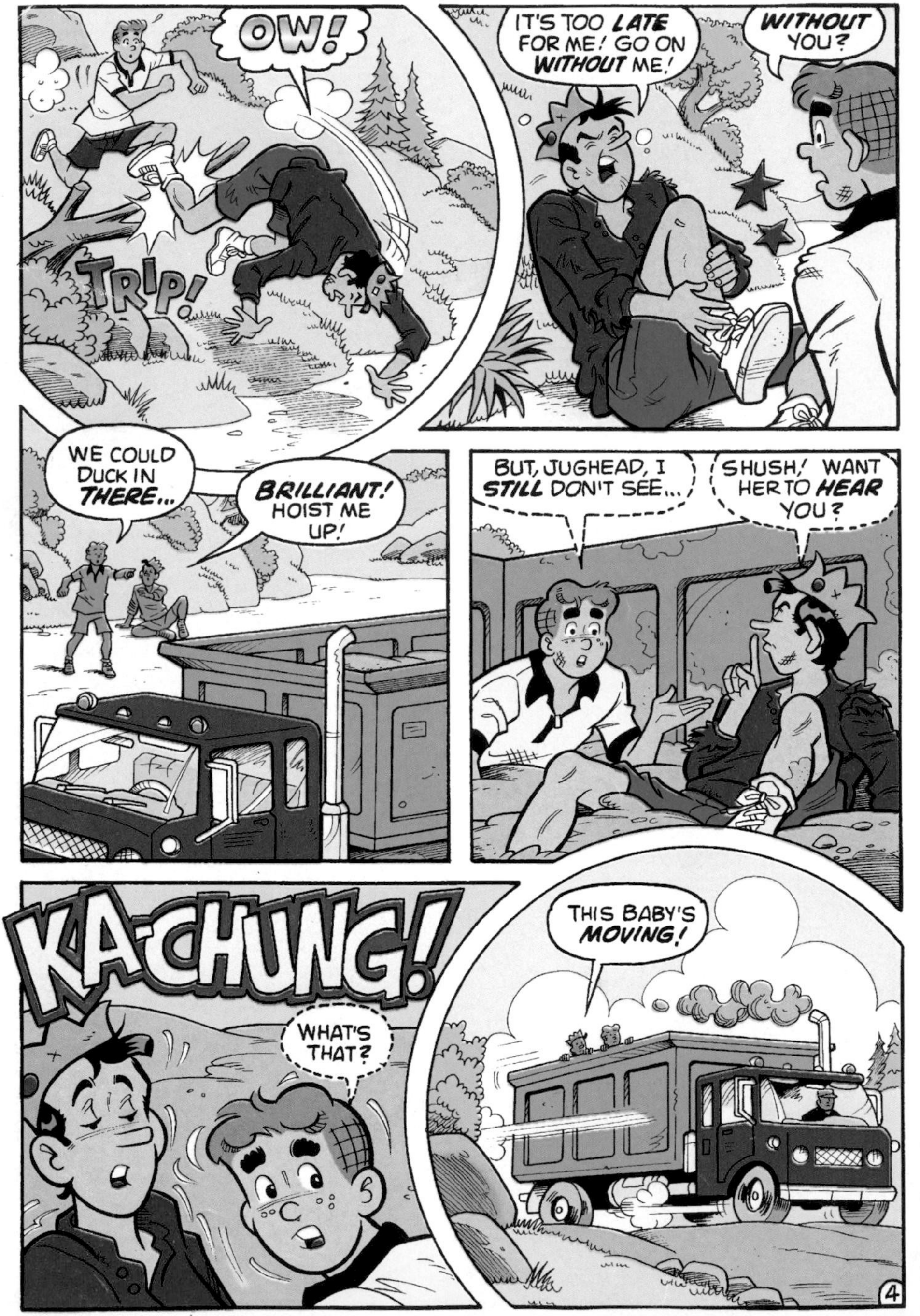
OW!
TRIP!
IT'S TOO LATE FOR ME! GO ON WITHOUT ME!
WITHOUT YOU?
WE COULD DUCK IN THERE...
BRILLIANT! HOIST ME UP!
BUT, JUGHEAD, I STILL DON'T SEE...
SHUSH! WANT HER TO HEAR YOU?
KA-CHUNG!
WHAT'S THAT?
THIS BABY'S MOVING!
4

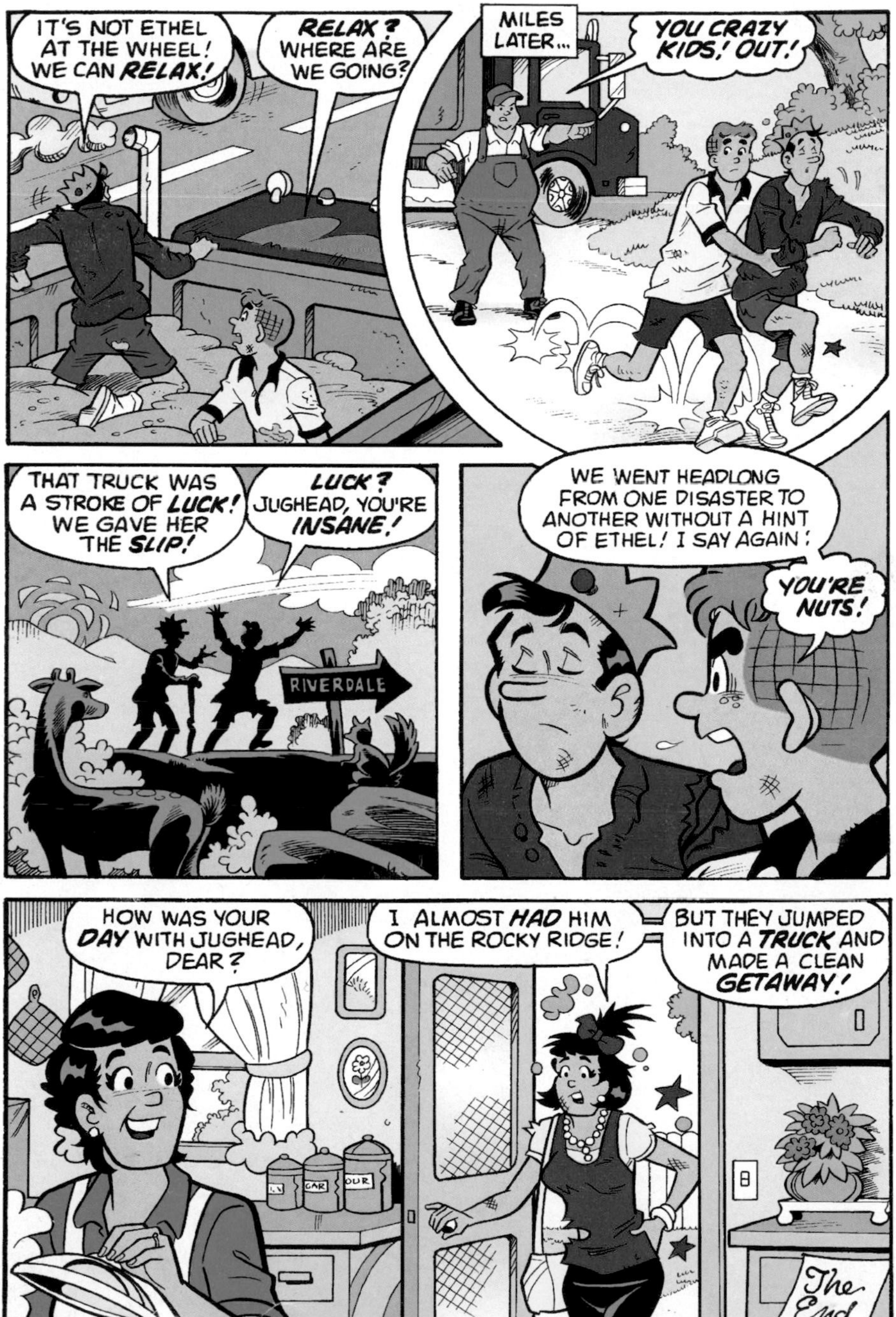
IT'S NOT ETHEL AT THE WHEEL! WE CAN RELAX!
RELAX? WHERE ARE WE GOING?
MILES LATER...
YOU CRAZY KIDS! OUT!
THAT TRUCK WAS A STROKE OF LUCK! WE GAVE HER THE SLIP!
LUCK? JUGHEAD, YOU'RE INSANE!
RIVERDALE
WE WENT HEADLONG FROM ONE DISASTER TO ANOTHER WITHOUT A HINT OF ETHEL! I SAY AGAIN:
YOU'RE NUTS!
HOW WAS YOUR DAY WITH JUGHEAD, DEAR?
I ALMOST HAD HIM ON THE ROCKY RIDGE!
BUT THEY JUMPED INTO A TRUCK AND MADE A CLEAN GETAWAY!
The End

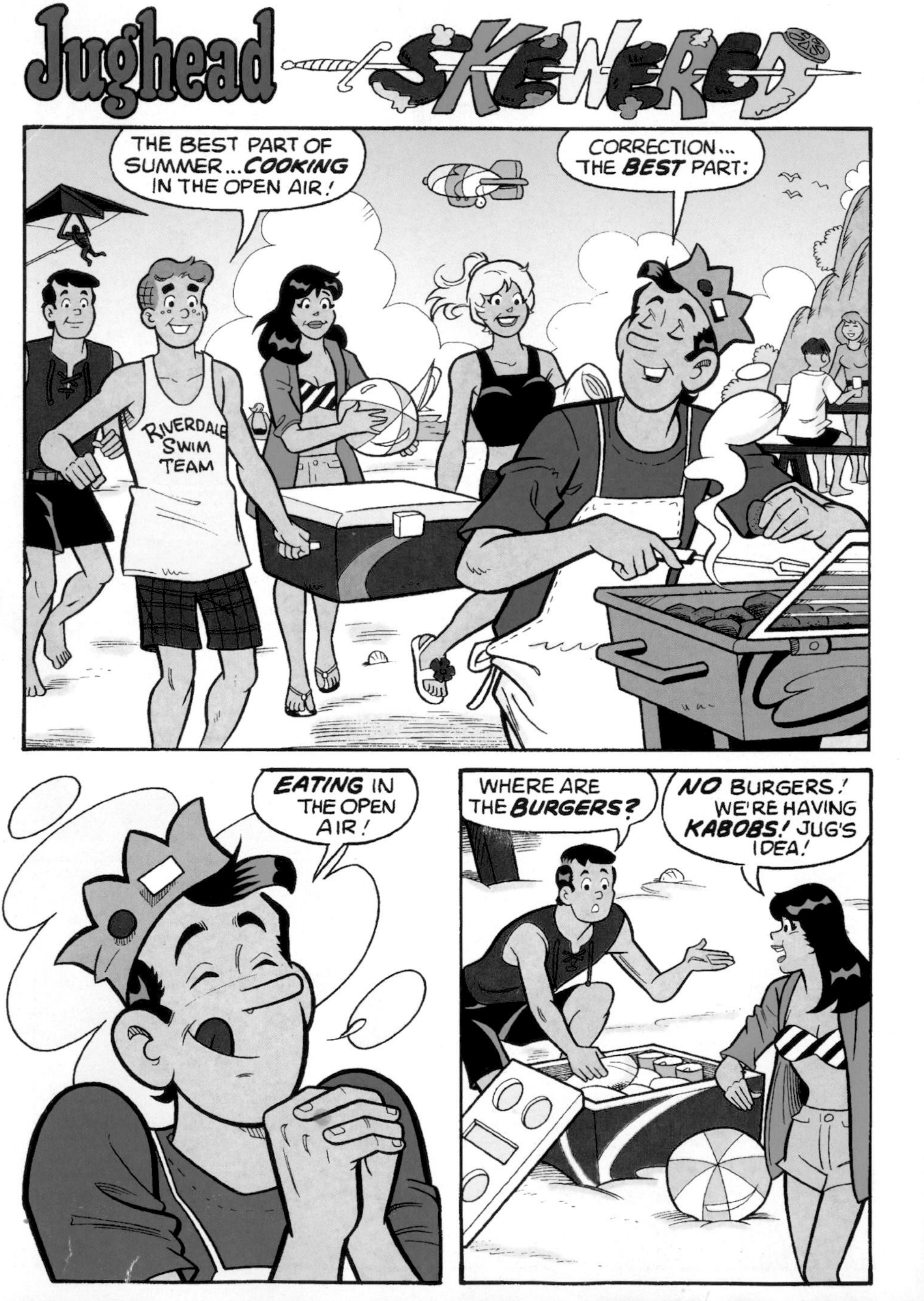
Jughead
SKEWERED
THE BEST PART OF SUMMER...COOKING IN THE OPEN AIR!
CORRECTION... THE BEST PART:
RIVERDALE SWIM TEAM
EATING IN THE OPEN AIR!
WHERE ARE THE BURGERS?
NO BURGERS! WE'RE HAVING KABOBS! JUG'S IDEA!

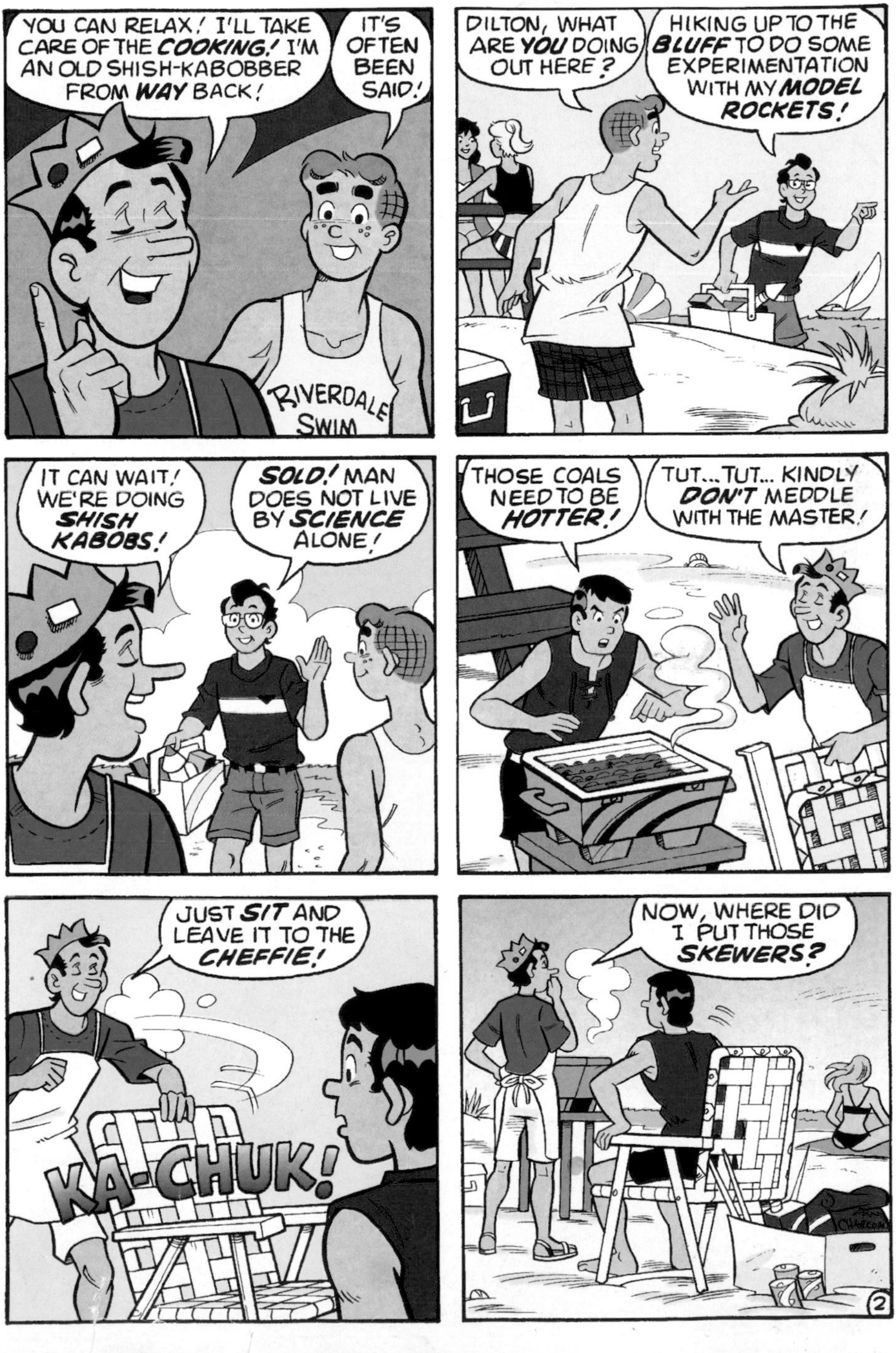
YOU CAN RELAX! I'LL TAKE CARE OF THE COOKING! I'M AN OLD SHISH-KABOBBER FROM WAY BACK!
IT'S OFTEN BEEN SAID!
RIVERDALE SWIM
DILTON, WHAT ARE YOU DOING OUT HERE?
HIKING UP TO THE BLUFF TO DO SOME EXPERIMENTATION WITH MY MODEL ROCKETS!
IT CAN WAIT! WE'RE DOING SHISH KABOBS!
SOLD! MAN DOES NOT LIVE BY SCIENCE ALONE!
THOSE COALS NEED TO BE HOTTER!
TUT...TUT... KINDLY DON'T MEDDLE WITH THE MASTER!
JUST SIT AND LEAVE IT TO THE CHEFFIE!
KA-CHUK!
NOW, WHERE DID I PUT THOSE SKEWERS?
2

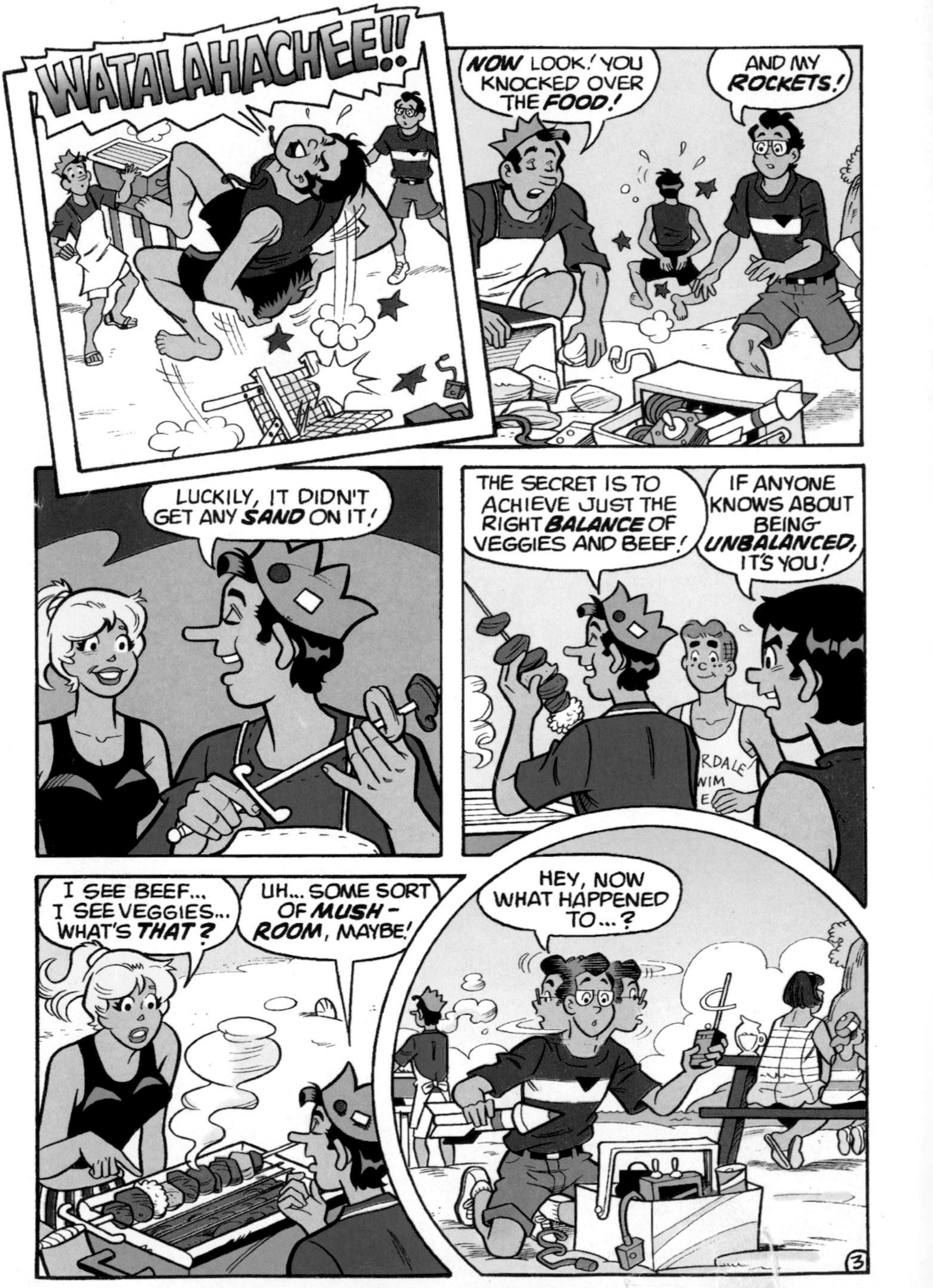
WATALAHACHEE!!
NOW LOOK! YOU KNOCKED OVER THE FOOD!
AND MY ROCKETS!
LUCKILY, IT DIDN'T GET ANY SAND ON IT!
THE SECRET IS TO ACHIEVE JUST THE RIGHT BALANCE OF VEGGIES AND BEEF!
IF ANYONE KNOWS ABOUT BEING-UNBALANCED, IT'S YOU!
I SEE BEEF... I SEE VEGGIES... WHAT'S THAT?
UH... SOME SORT OF MUSH-ROOM, MAYBE!
HEY, NOW WHAT HAPPENED TO...?
3

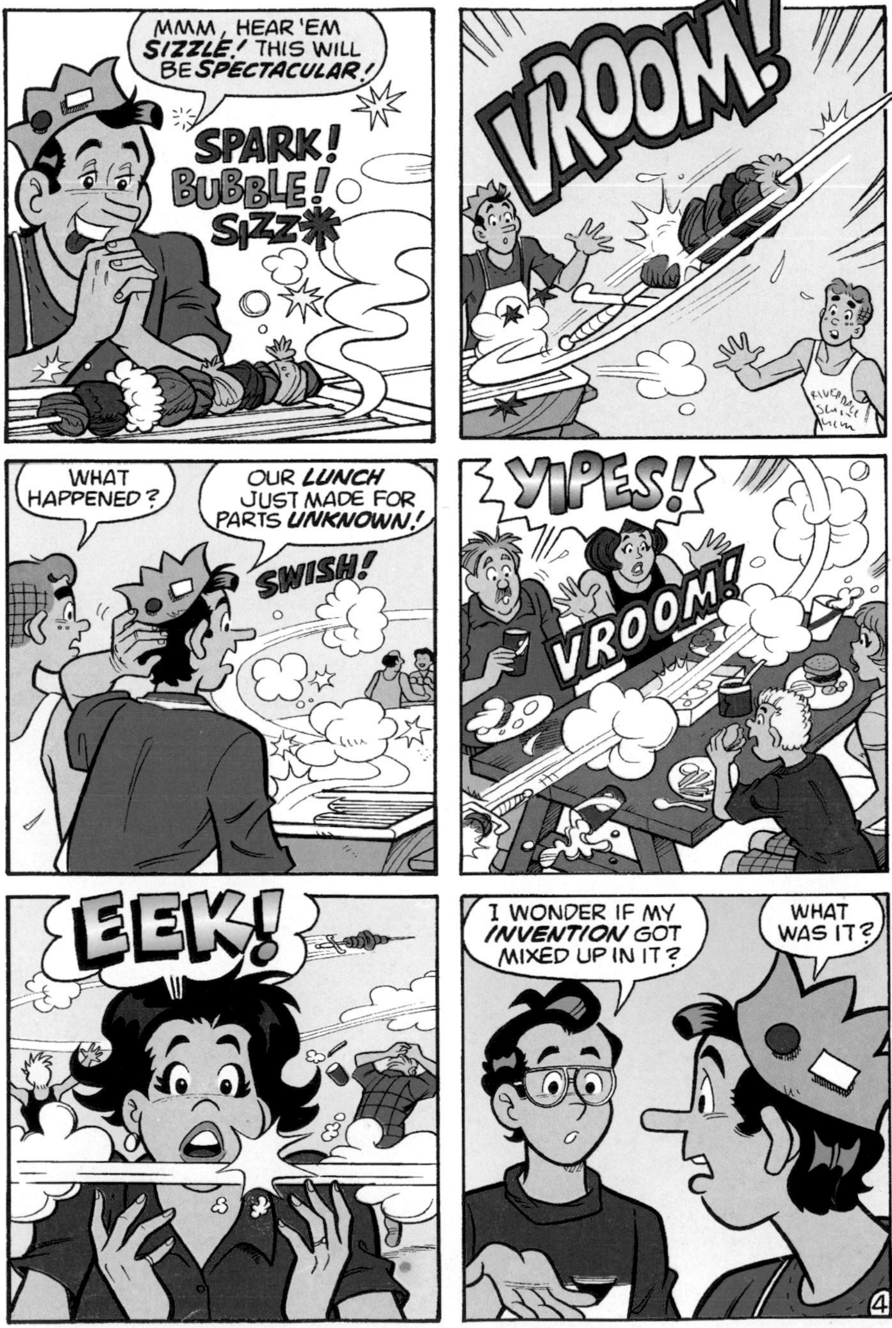
MMM, HEAR 'EM SIZZLE! THIS WILL BE SPECTACULAR!
SPARK! BUBBLE! SIZZ*
VROOM!
WHAT HAPPENED?
OUR LUNCH JUST MADE FOR PARTS UNKNOWN!
SWISH!
YIPES!
VROOM!
EEK!
I WONDER IF MY INVENTION GOT MIXED UP IN IT?
WHAT WAS IT?
4

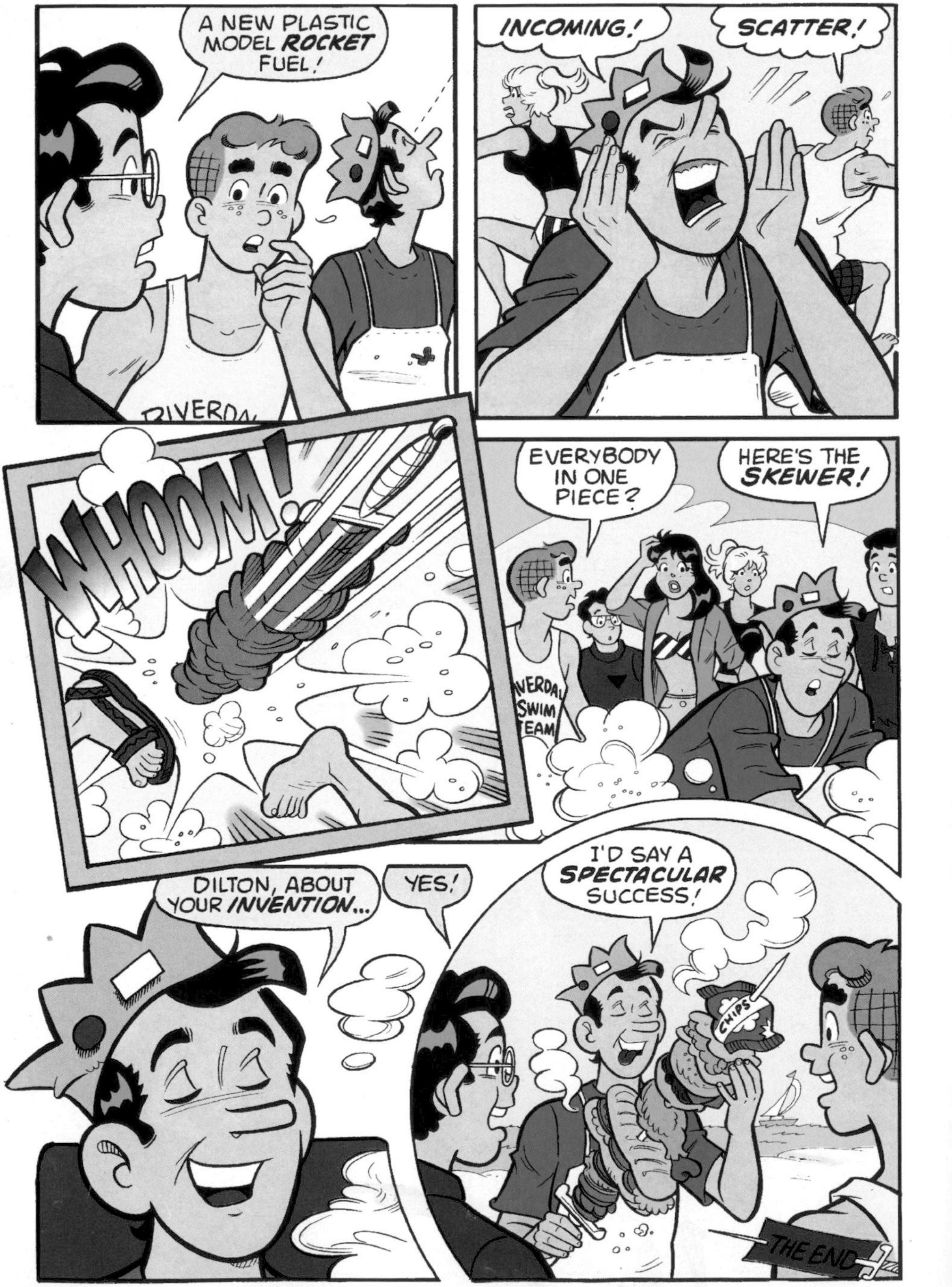
A NEW PLASTIC MODEL ROCKET FUEL!
RIVERDA
INCOMING!
SCATTER!
WHOOM!
EVERYBODY IN ONE PIECE?
HERE'S THE SKEWER!
VERDA SWIM TEAM
DILTON, ABOUT YOUR INVENTION...
YES!
I'D SAY A SPECTACULAR SUCCESS!
CHIPS
THE END

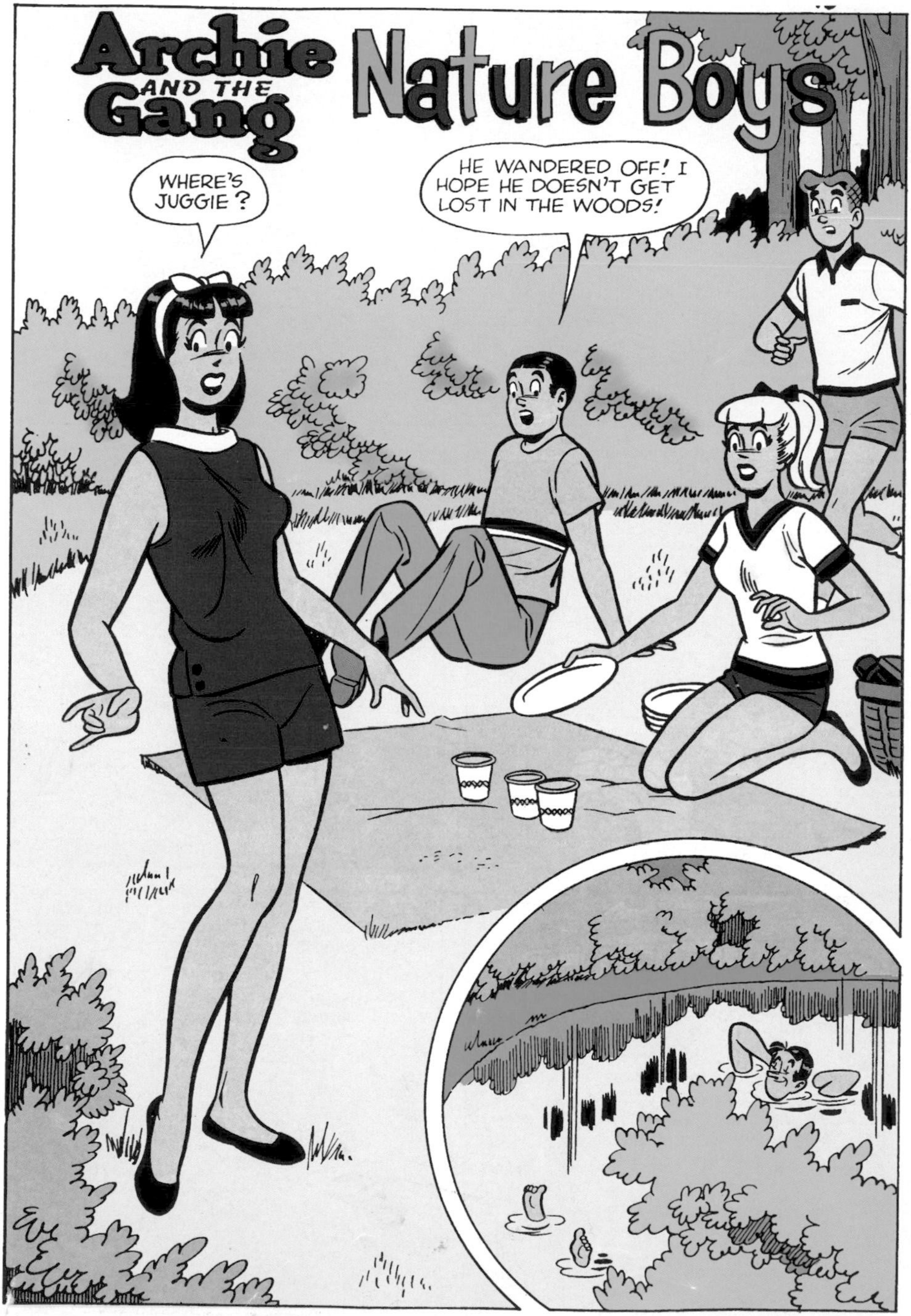
Archie AND THE Gang
Nature Boys
WHERE'S JUGGIE ?
HE WANDERED OFF! I HOPE HE DOESN'T GET LOST IN THE WOODS!

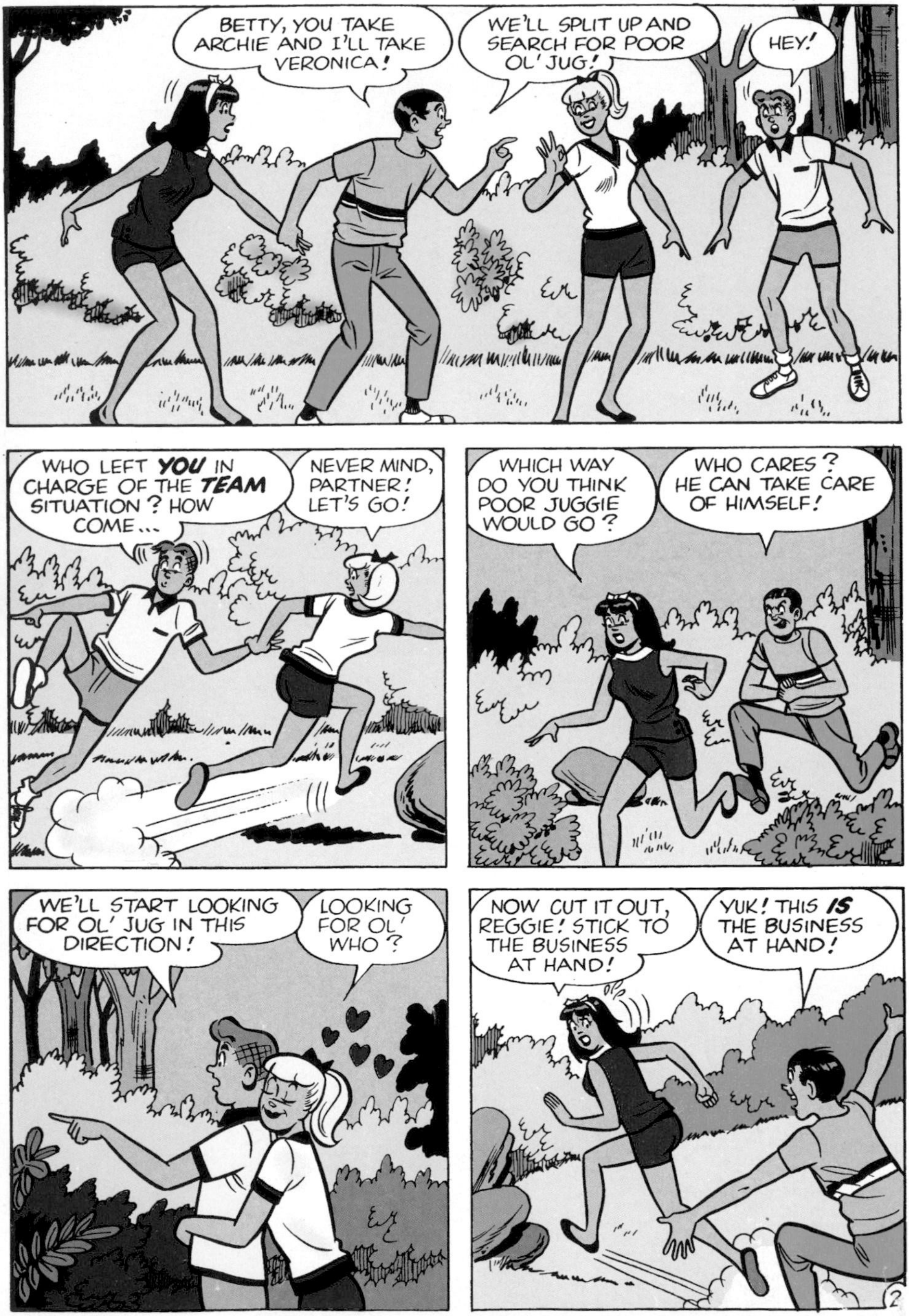
BETTY, YOU TAKE ARCHIE AND I'LL TAKE VERONICA!
WE'LL SPLIT UP AND SEARCH FOR POOR OL' JUG!
HEY!
WHO LEFT YOU IN CHARGE OF THE TEAM SITUATION? HOW COME...
NEVER MIND, PARTNER! LET'S GO!
WHICH WAY DO YOU THINK POOR JUGGIE WOULD GO?
WHO CARES? HE CAN TAKE CARE OF HIMSELF!
WE'LL START LOOKING FOR OL' JUG IN THIS DIRECTION!
LOOKING FOR OL' WHO?
NOW CUT IT OUT, REGGIE! STICK TO THE BUSINESS AT HAND!
YUK! THIS IS THE BUSINESS AT HAND!
2

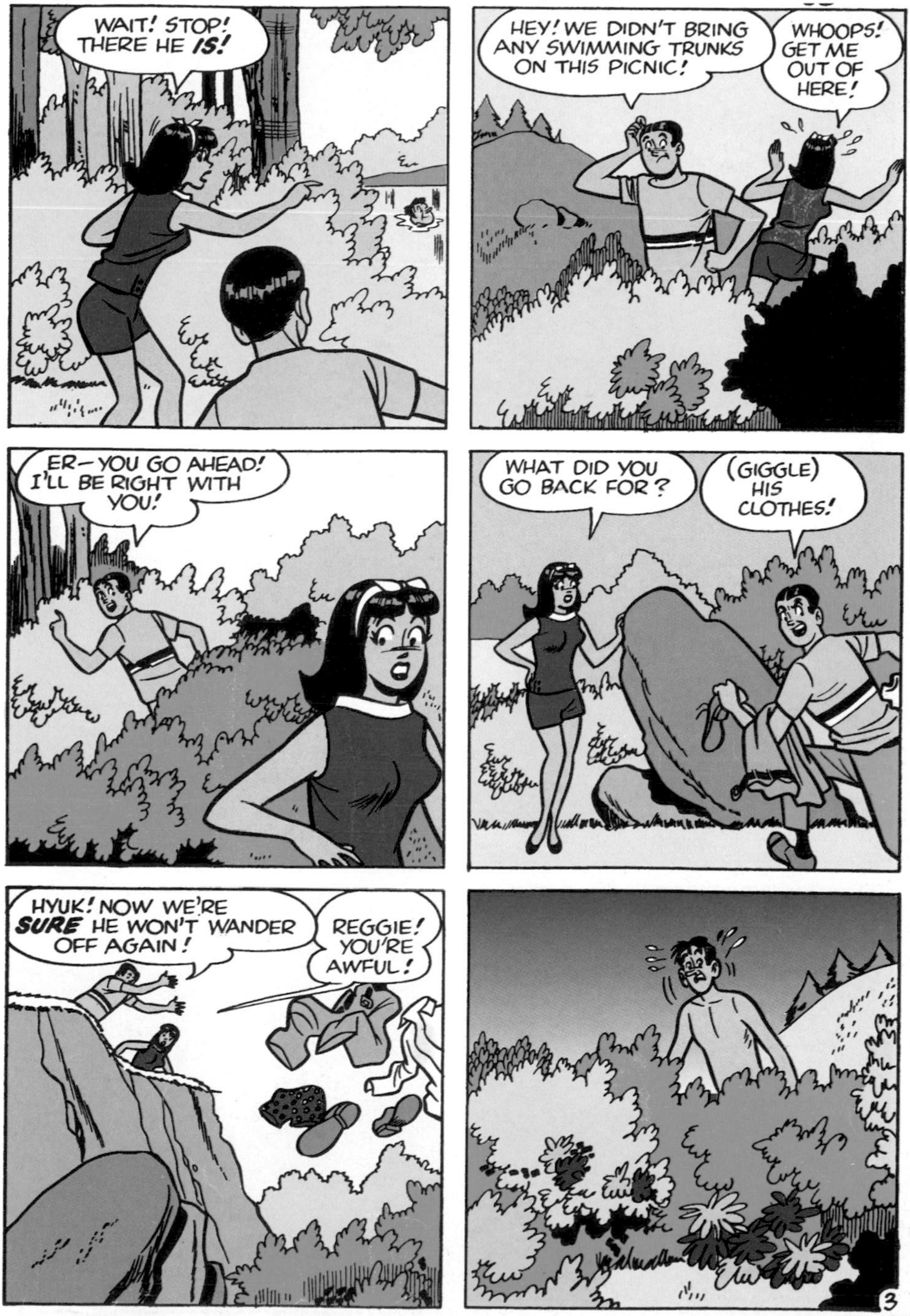
WAIT! STOP! THERE HE IS!
HEY! WE DIDN'T BRING ANY SWIMMING TRUNKS ON THIS PICNIC!
WHOOPS! GET ME OUT OF HERE!
ER—YOU GO AHEAD! I'LL BE RIGHT WITH YOU!
WHAT DID YOU GO BACK FOR?
(GIGGLE) HIS CLOTHES!
HYUK! NOW WE'RE SURE HE WON'T WANDER OFF AGAIN!
REGGIE! YOU'RE AWFUL!
3

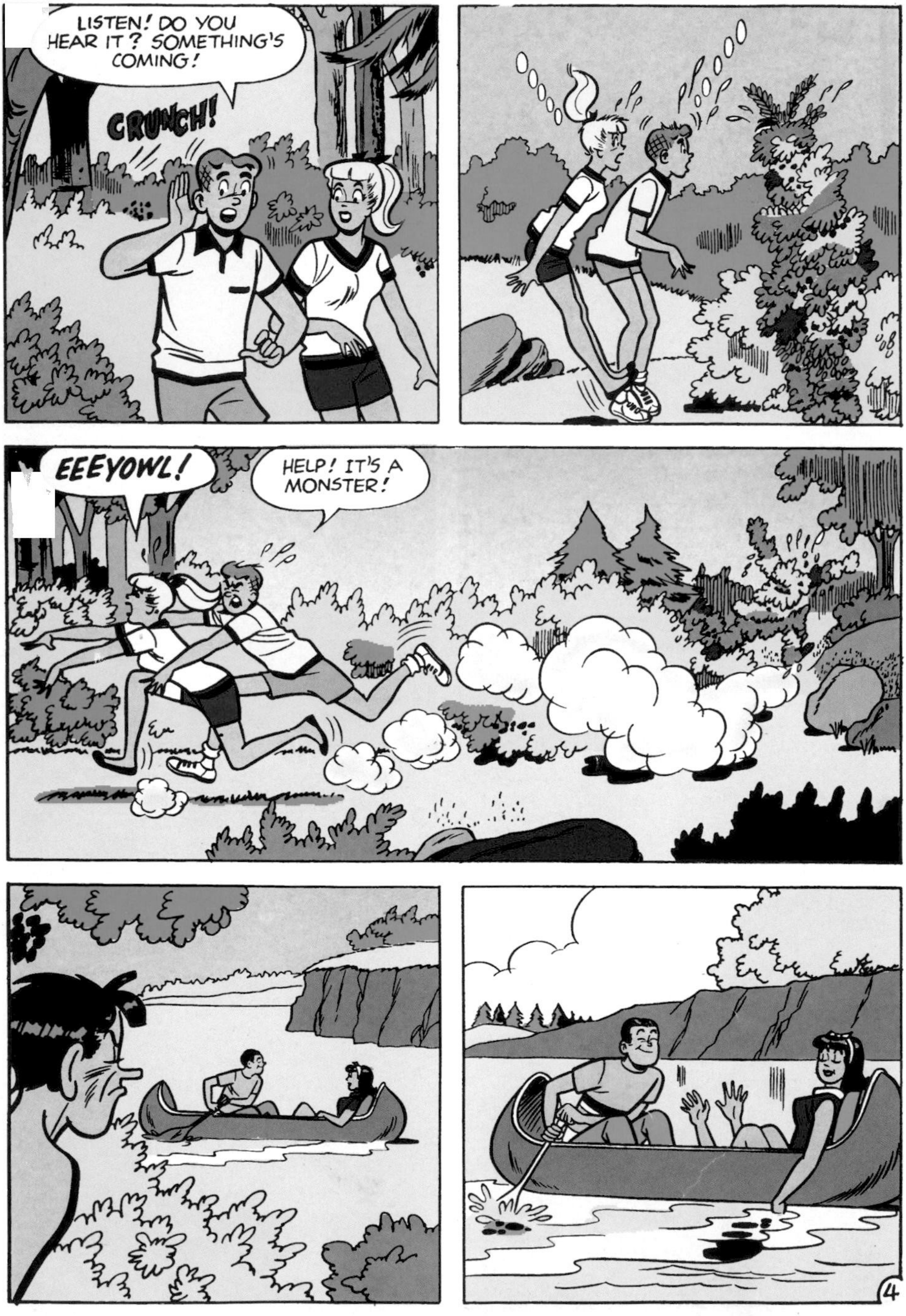
LISTEN! DO YOU HEAR IT? SOMETHING'S COMING!
CRUNCH!
EEEYOWL!
HELP! IT'S A MONSTER!
4

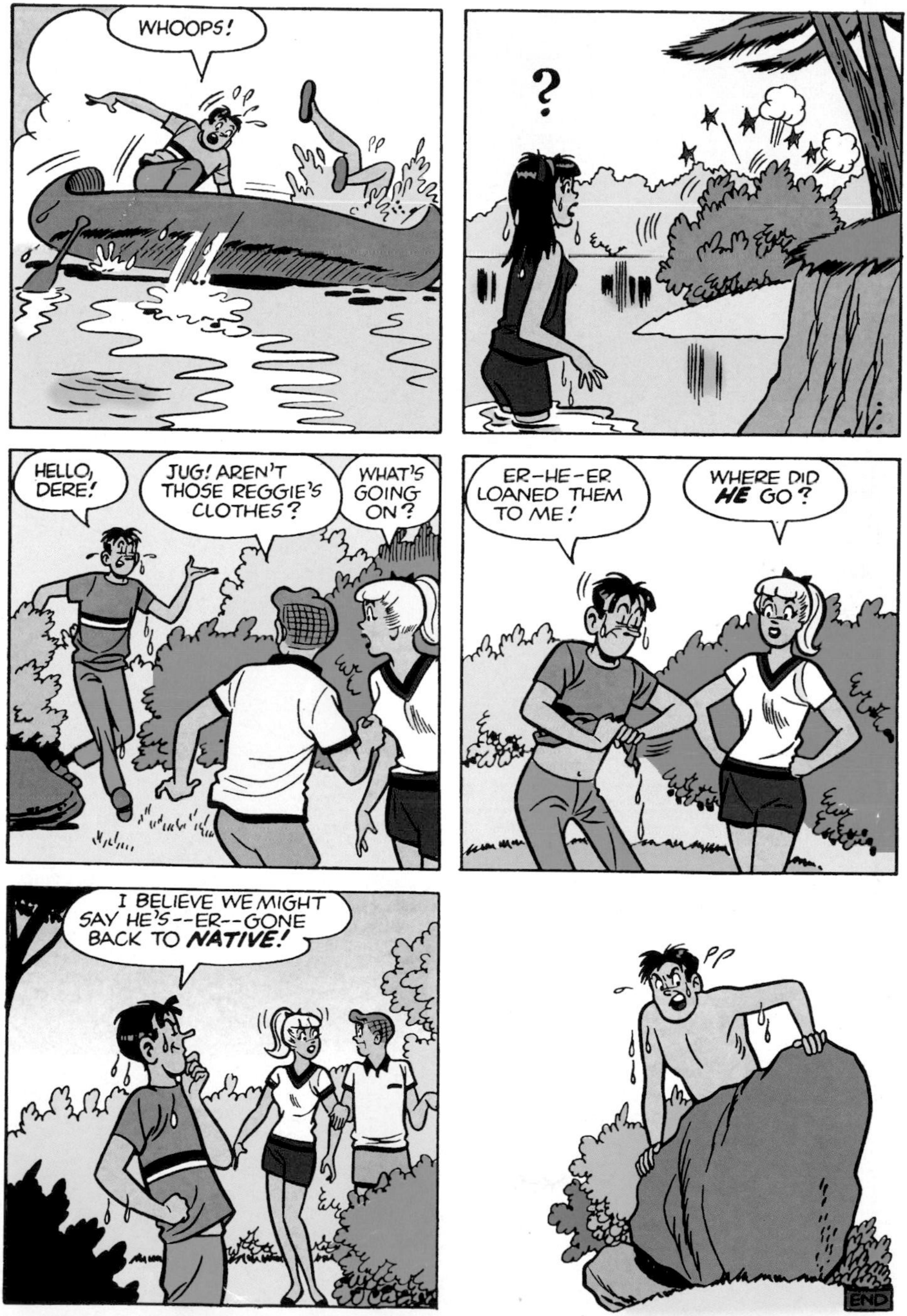
WHOOPS!
?
HELLO, DERE!
JUG! AREN'T THOSE REGGIE'S CLOTHES?
WHAT'S GOING ON?
ER-HE-ER LOANED THEM TO ME!
WHERE DID **HE** GO?
I BELIEVE WE MIGHT SAY HE'S--ER--GONE BACK TO **NATIVE**!
END

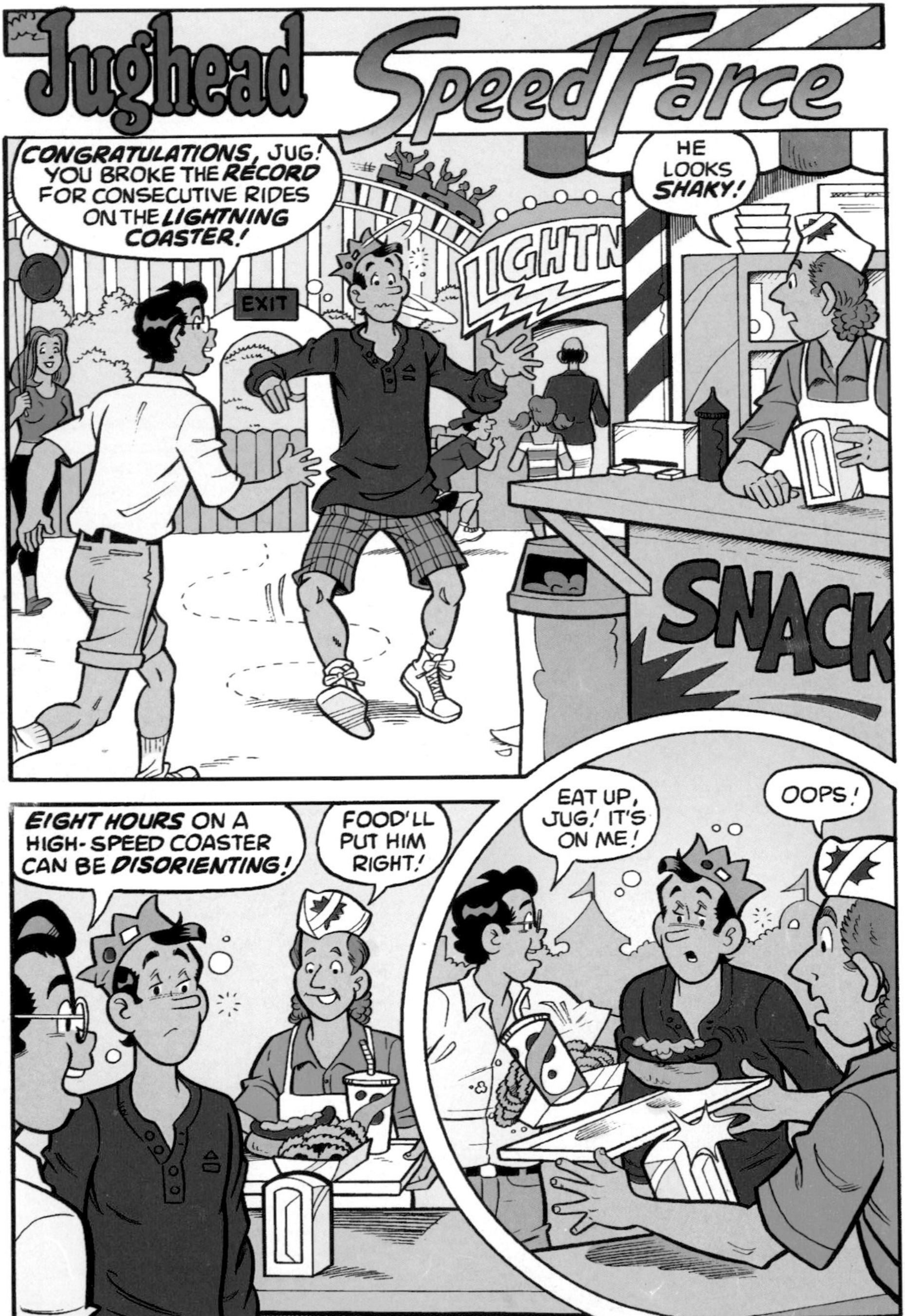
Jughead
Speed Farce
CONGRATULATIONS, JUG! YOU BROKE THE RECORD FOR CONSECUTIVE RIDES ON THE LIGHTNING COASTER!
EXIT
LIGHTN
HE LOOKS SHAKY!
SNACK
EIGHT HOURS ON A HIGH-SPEED COASTER CAN BE DISORIENTING!
FOOD'LL PUT HIM RIGHT!
EAT UP, JUG! IT'S ON ME!
OOPS!

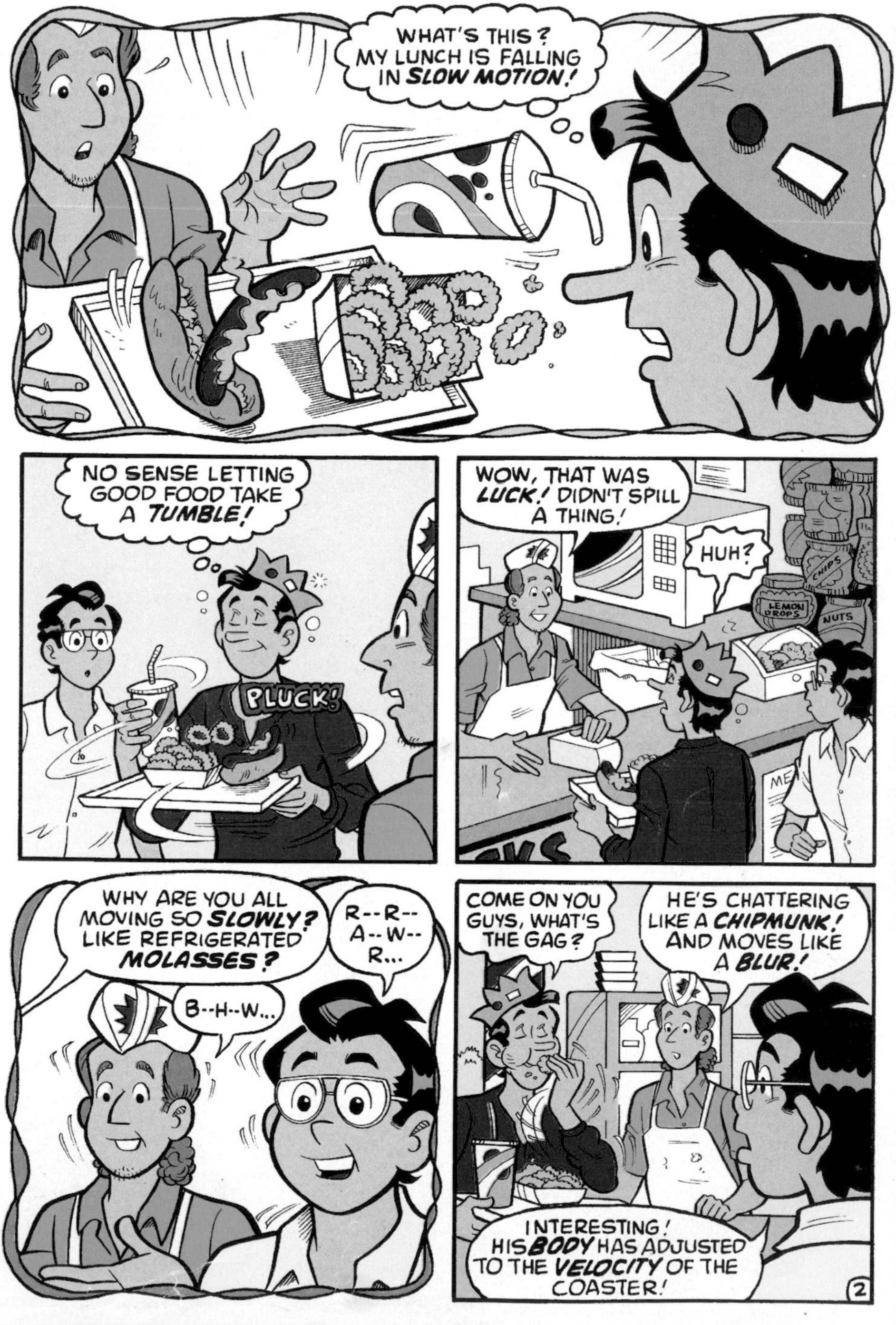
WHAT'S THIS? MY LUNCH IS FALLING IN SLOW MOTION!
NO SENSE LETTING GOOD FOOD TAKE A TUMBLE!
PLUCK!
WOW, THAT WAS LUCK! DIDN'T SPILL A THING!
HUH?
LEMON DROPS
CHIPS
NUTS
WHY ARE YOU ALL MOVING SO SLOWLY? LIKE REFRIGERATED MOLASSES?
R--R-- A--W-- R...
B--H--W...
COME ON YOU GUYS, WHAT'S THE GAG?
HE'S CHATTERING LIKE A CHIPMUNK! AND MOVES LIKE A BLUR!
INTERESTING! HIS BODY HAS ADJUSTED TO THE VELOCITY OF THE COASTER!
2

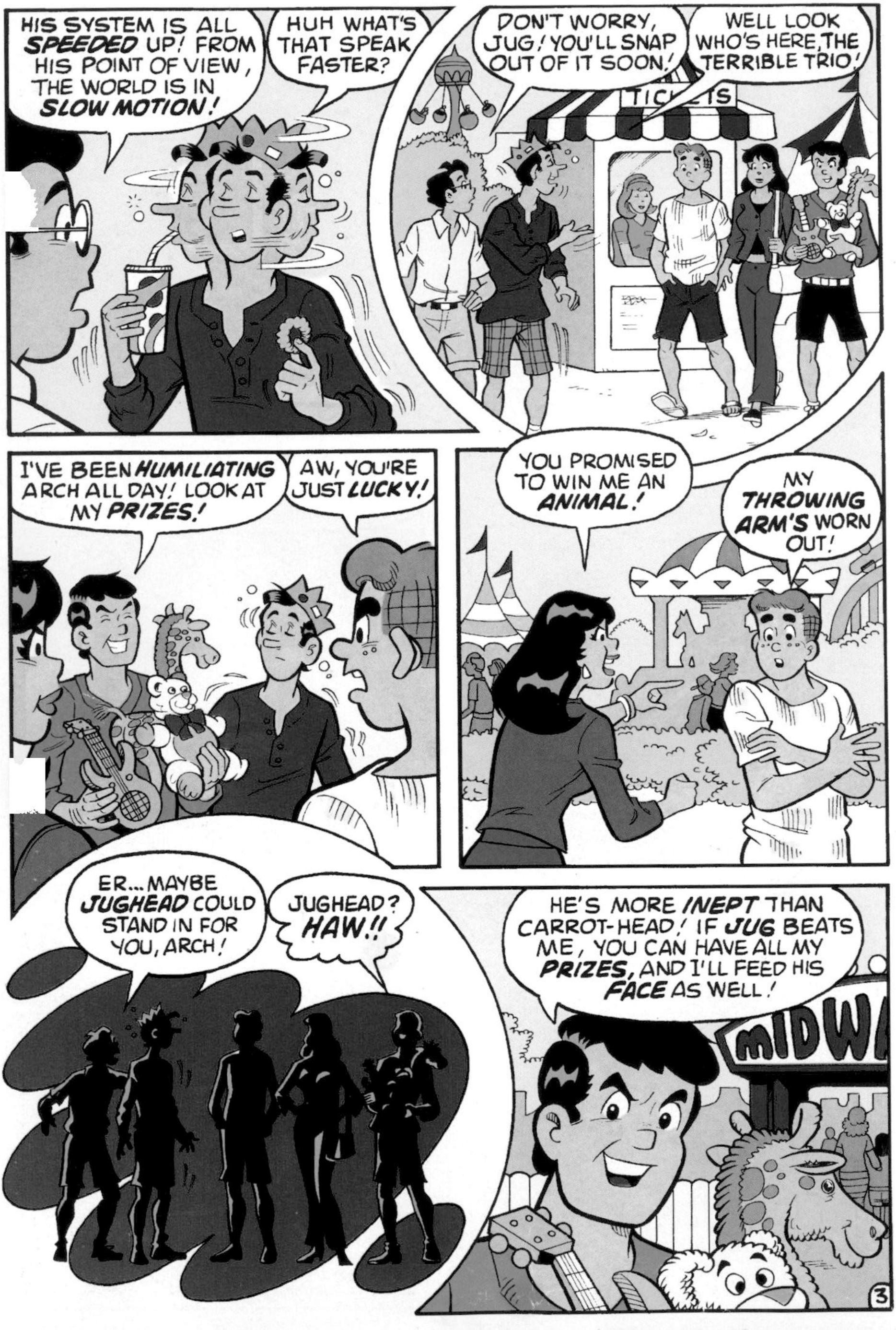
HIS SYSTEM IS ALL SPEEDED UP! FROM HIS POINT OF VIEW, THE WORLD IS IN SLOW MOTION!
HUH WHAT'S THAT SPEAK FASTER?
DON'T WORRY, JUG! YOU'LL SNAP OUT OF IT SOON!
WELL LOOK WHO'S HERE, THE TERRIBLE TRIO!
TICKETS
I'VE BEEN HUMILIATING ARCH ALL DAY! LOOK AT MY PRIZES!
AW, YOU'RE JUST LUCKY!
YOU PROMISED TO WIN ME AN ANIMAL!
MY THROWING ARM'S WORN OUT!
ER... MAYBE JUGHEAD COULD STAND IN FOR YOU, ARCH!
JUGHEAD? HAW!!
HE'S MORE INEPT THAN CARROT-HEAD! IF JUG BEATS ME, YOU CAN HAVE ALL MY PRIZES, AND I'LL FEED HIS FACE AS WELL!
3

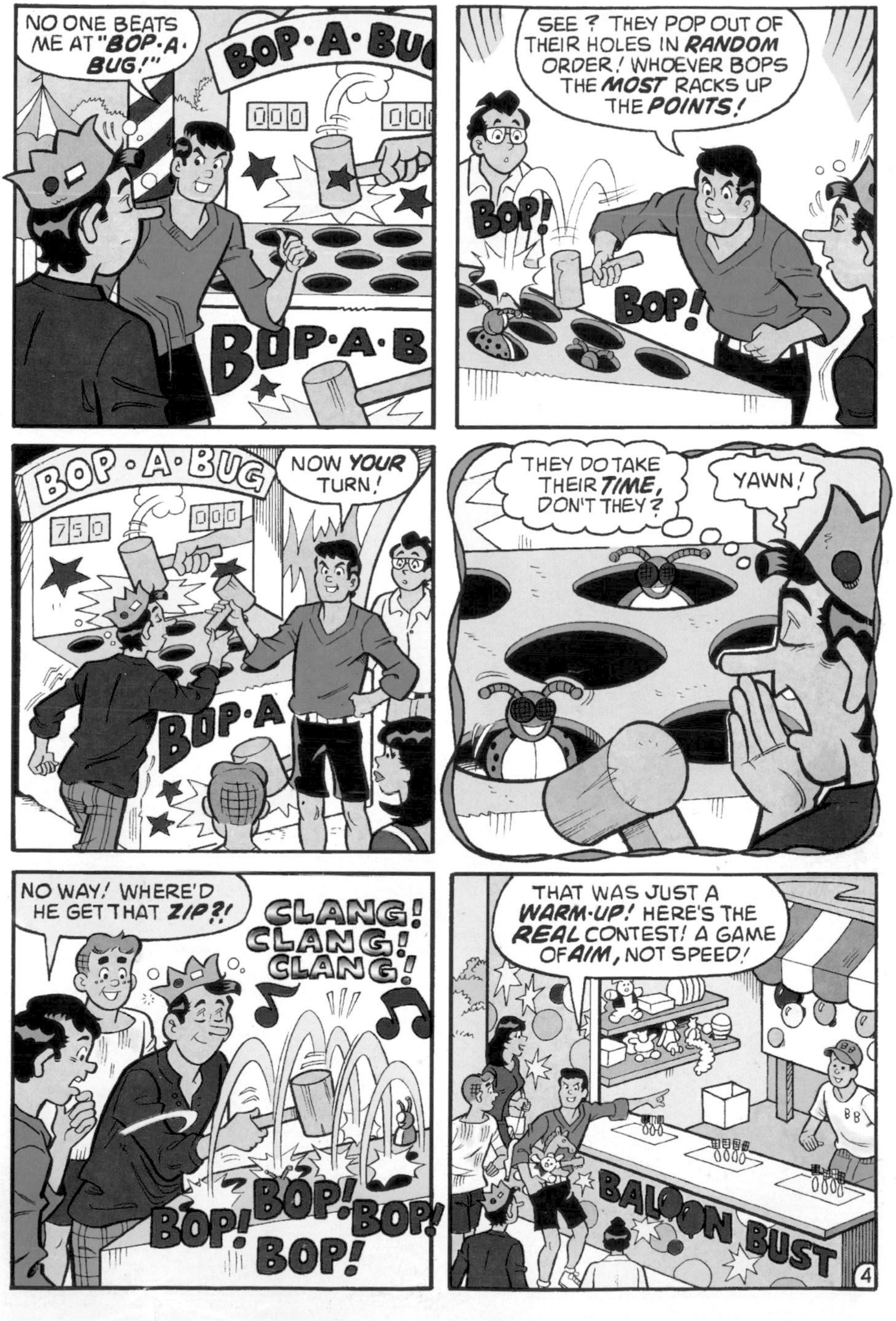
NO ONE BEATS ME AT "BOP-A-BUG!"
BOP-A-BUG
BOP-A-B
SEE? THEY POP OUT OF THEIR HOLES IN RANDOM ORDER! WHOEVER BOPS THE MOST RACKS UP THE POINTS!
BOP!
BOP!
BOP-A-BUG
750
000
NOW YOUR TURN!
BOP-A
THEY DO TAKE THEIR TIME, DON'T THEY?
YAWN!
NO WAY! WHERE'D HE GET THAT ZIP?!
CLANG! CLANG! CLANG!
BOP! BOP! BOP! BOP!
THAT WAS JUST A WARM-UP! HERE'S THE REAL CONTEST! A GAME OF AIM, NOT SPEED!
BB
BALOON BUST
4

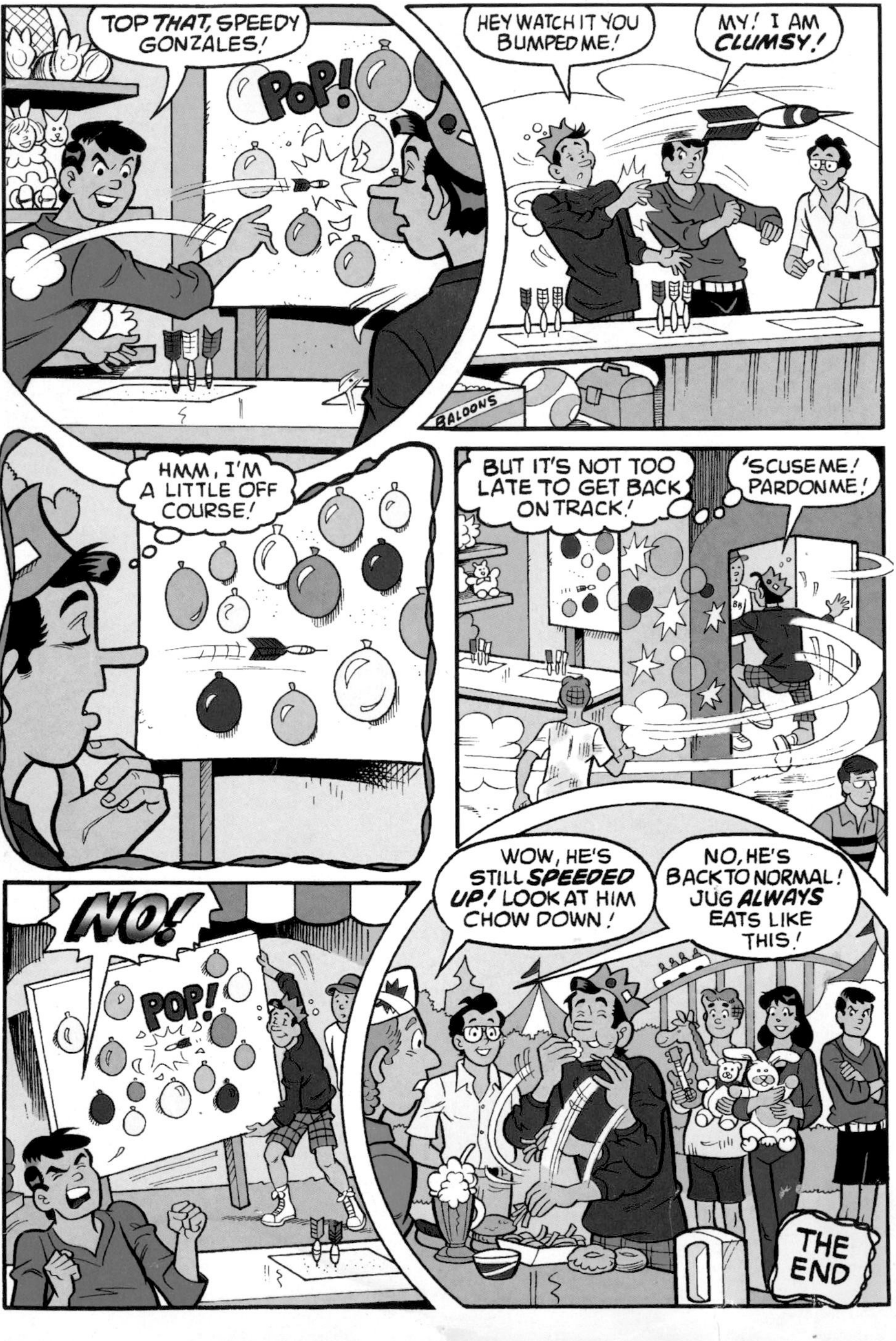
TOP *THAT*, SPEEDY GONZALES!
POP!
HEY WATCH IT YOU BUMPED ME!
MY! I AM *CLUMSY*!
BALOONS
HMM, I'M A LITTLE OFF COURSE!
BUT IT'S NOT TOO LATE TO GET BACK ON TRACK!
'SCUSE ME! PARDON ME!
NO!
POP!
WOW, HE'S STILL *SPEEDED UP!* LOOK AT HIM CHOW DOWN!
NO, HE'S BACK TO NORMAL! JUG *ALWAYS* EATS LIKE THIS!
THE END

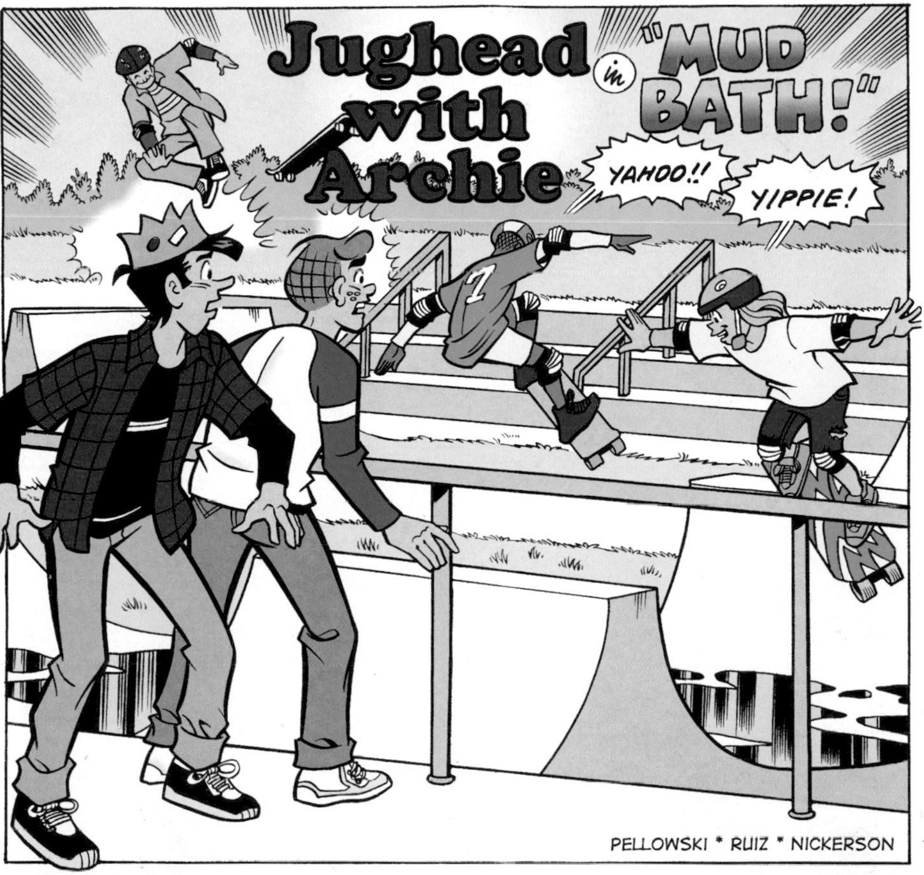
Jughead with Archie in "MUD BATH!"
YAHOO!!
YIPPIE!
PELLOWSKI * RUIZ * NICKERSON

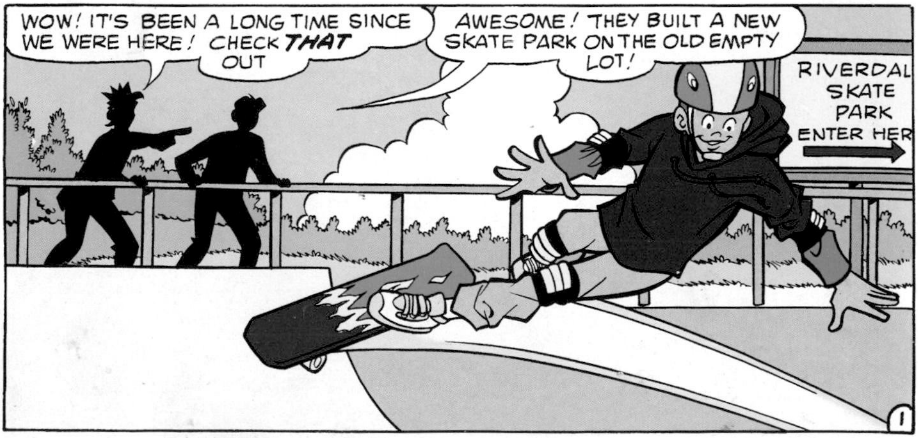
WOW! IT'S BEEN A LONG TIME SINCE WE WERE HERE! CHECK THAT OUT
AWESOME! THEY BUILT A NEW SKATE PARK ON THE OLD EMPTY LOT!
RIVERDAL SKATE PARK ENTER HER
1

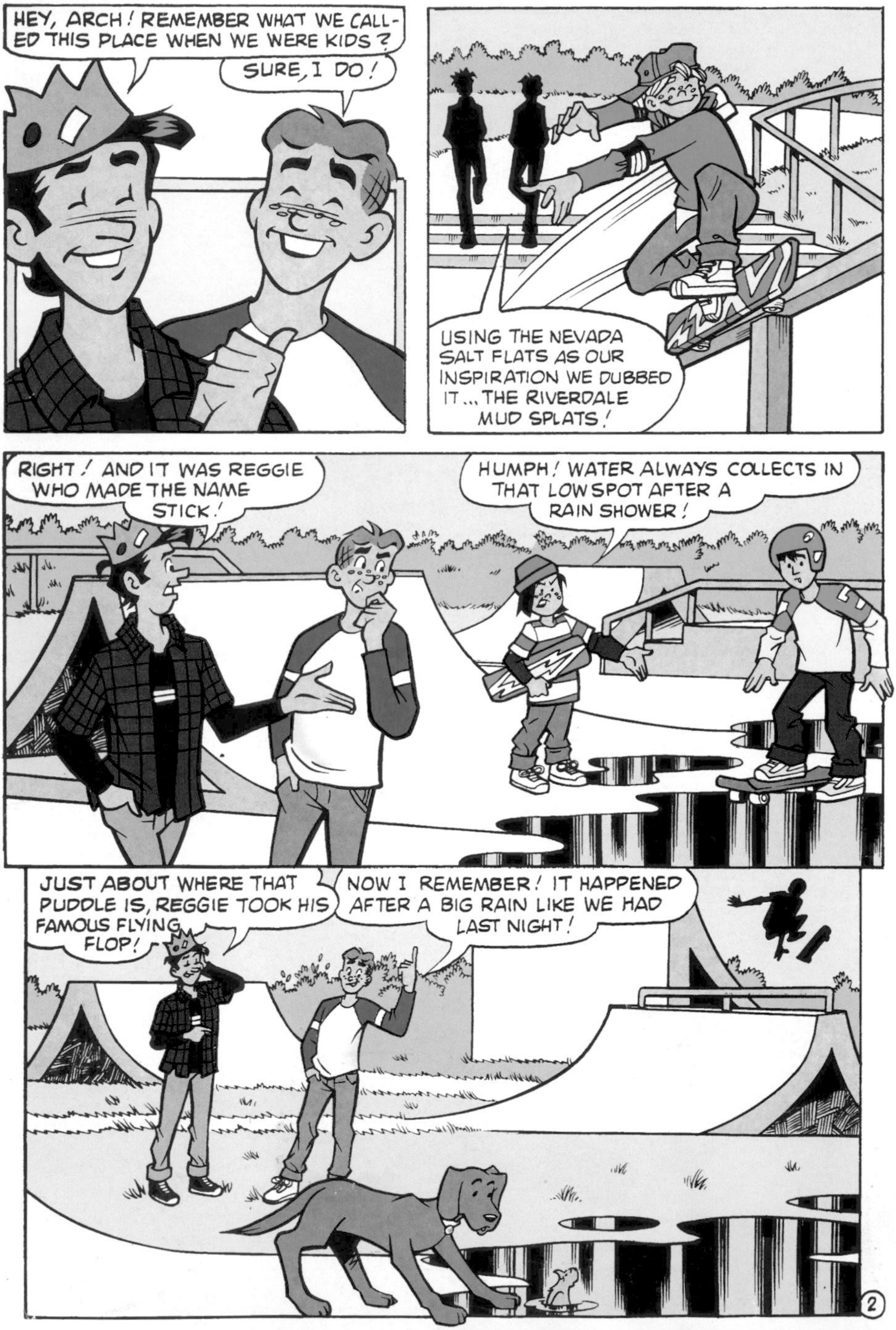
HEY, ARCH! REMEMBER WHAT WE CALL-ED THIS PLACE WHEN WE WERE KIDS?
SURE, I DO!
USING THE NEVADA SALT FLATS AS OUR INSPIRATION WE DUBBED IT... THE RIVERDALE MUD SPLATS!
RIGHT! AND IT WAS REGGIE WHO MADE THE NAME STICK!
HUMPH! WATER ALWAYS COLLECTS IN THAT LOW SPOT AFTER A RAIN SHOWER!
JUST ABOUT WHERE THAT PUDDLE IS, REGGIE TOOK HIS FAMOUS FLYING FLOP!
NOW I REMEMBER! IT HAPPENED AFTER A BIG RAIN LIKE WE HAD LAST NIGHT!
2

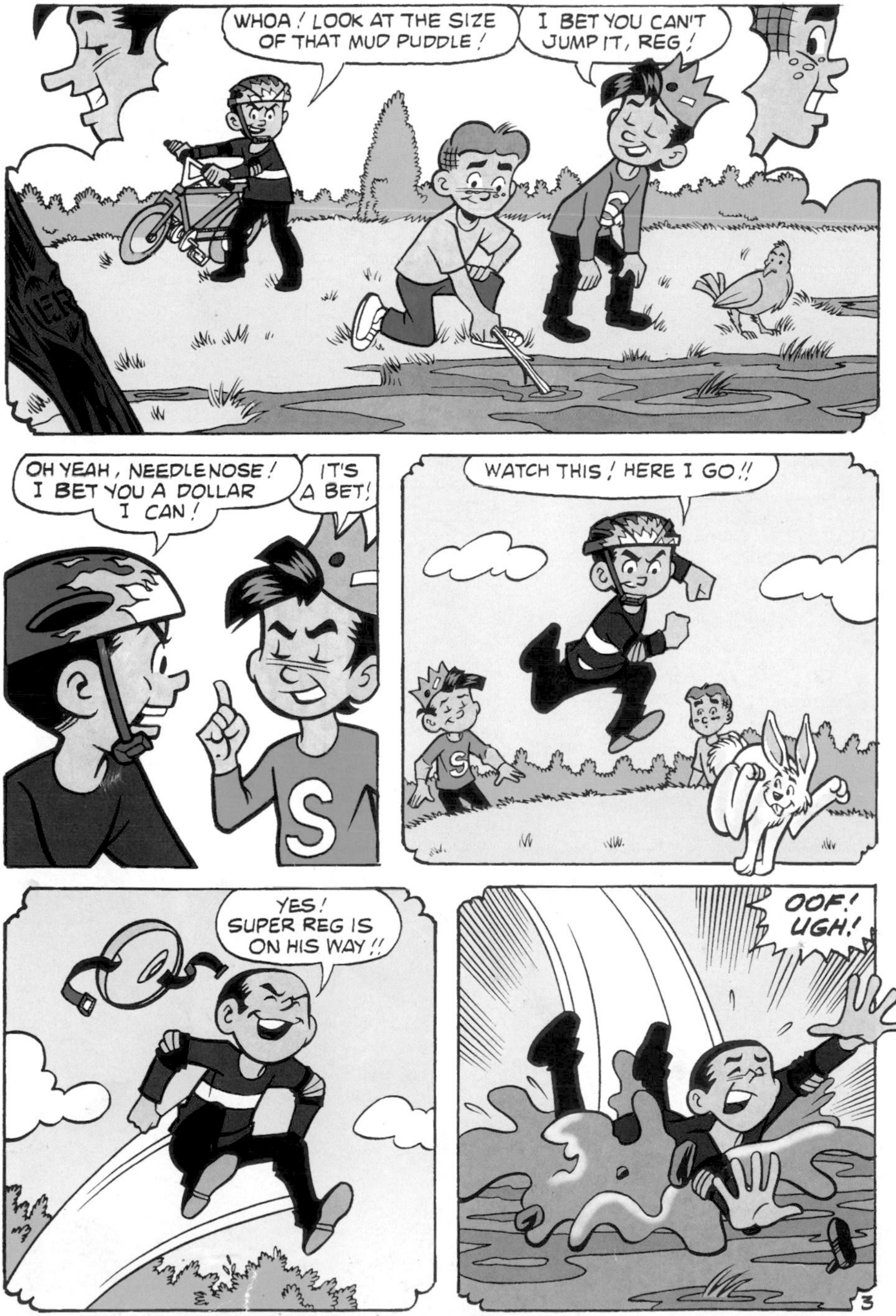
WHOA! LOOK AT THE SIZE OF THAT MUD PUDDLE!
I BET YOU CAN'T JUMP IT, REG!
OH YEAH, NEEDLENOSE! I BET YOU A DOLLAR I CAN!
IT'S A BET!
WATCH THIS! HERE I GO!!
YES! SUPER REG IS ON HIS WAY!!
OOF! UGH!
3

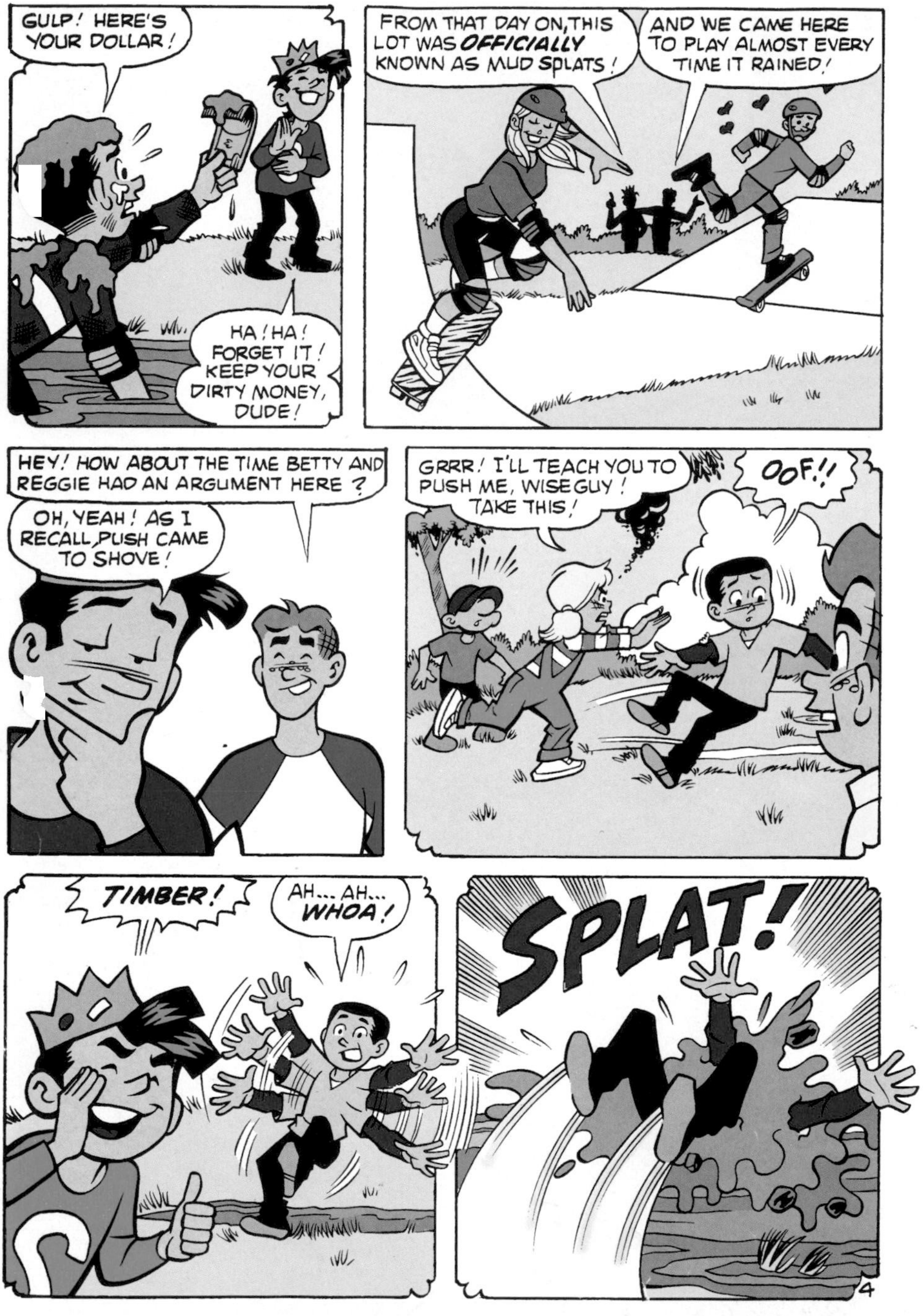
GULP! HERE'S YOUR DOLLAR!
HA! HA! FORGET IT! KEEP YOUR DIRTY MONEY, DUDE!
FROM THAT DAY ON, THIS LOT WAS OFFICIALLY KNOWN AS MUD SPLATS!
AND WE CAME HERE TO PLAY ALMOST EVERY TIME IT RAINED!
HEY! HOW ABOUT THE TIME BETTY AND REGGIE HAD AN ARGUMENT HERE?
OH, YEAH! AS I RECALL, PUSH CAME TO SHOVE!
GRRR! I'LL TEACH YOU TO PUSH ME, WISEGUY! TAKE THIS!
OOF!!
TIMBER!
AH... AH... WHOA!
SPLAT!
4

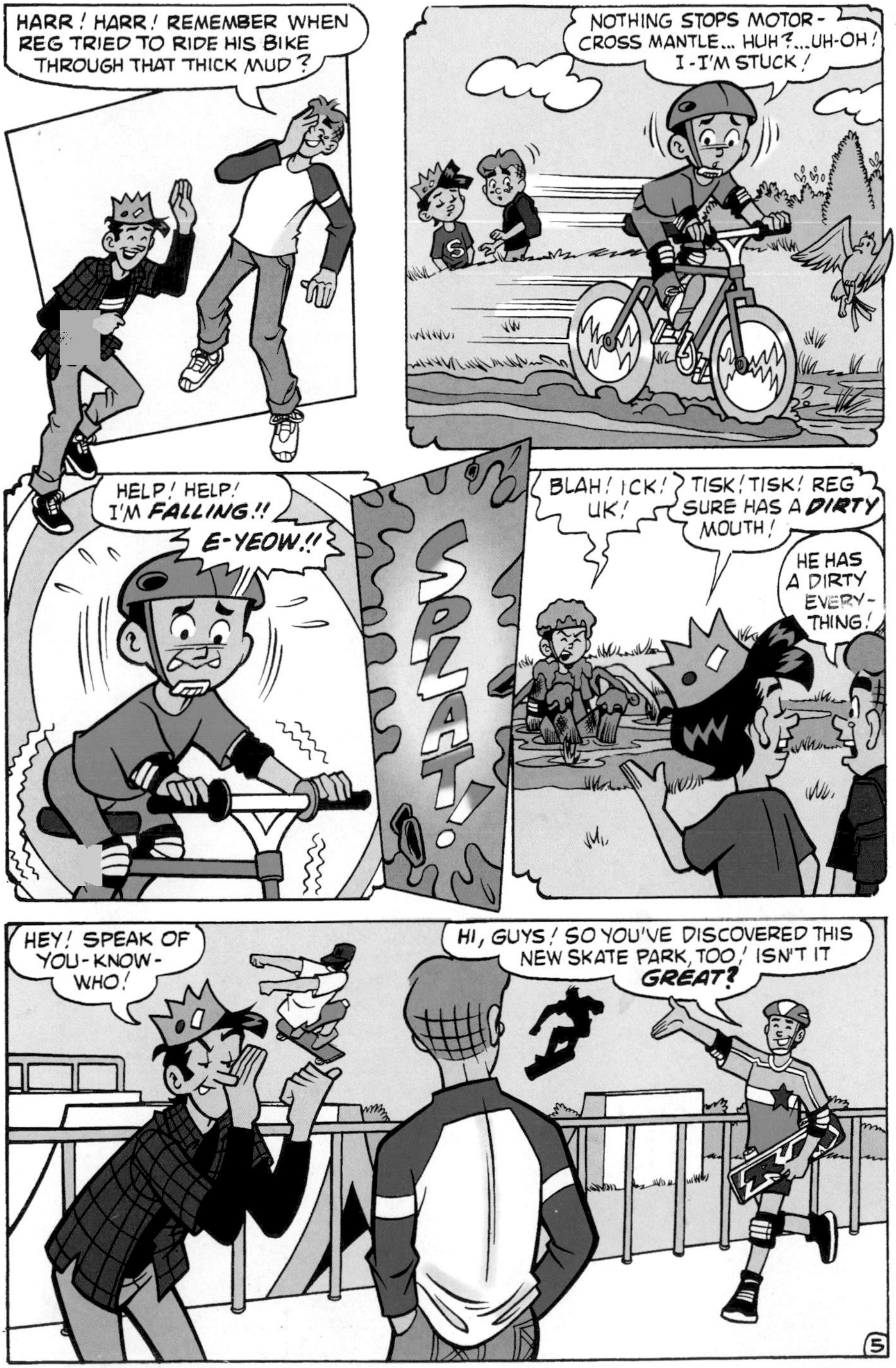
HARR! HARR! REMEMBER WHEN REG TRIED TO RIDE HIS BIKE THROUGH THAT THICK MUD?
NOTHING STOPS MOTOR-CROSS MANTLE... HUH?...UH-OH! I-I'M STUCK!
HELP! HELP! I'M FALLING!!
E-YEOW!!
SPLAT!
BLAH! ICK! UK!
TISK! TISK! REG SURE HAS A DIRTY MOUTH!
HE HAS A DIRTY EVERY-THING!
HEY! SPEAK OF YOU-KNOW-WHO!
HI, GUYS! SO YOU'VE DISCOVERED THIS NEW SKATE PARK, TOO! ISN'T IT GREAT?
5

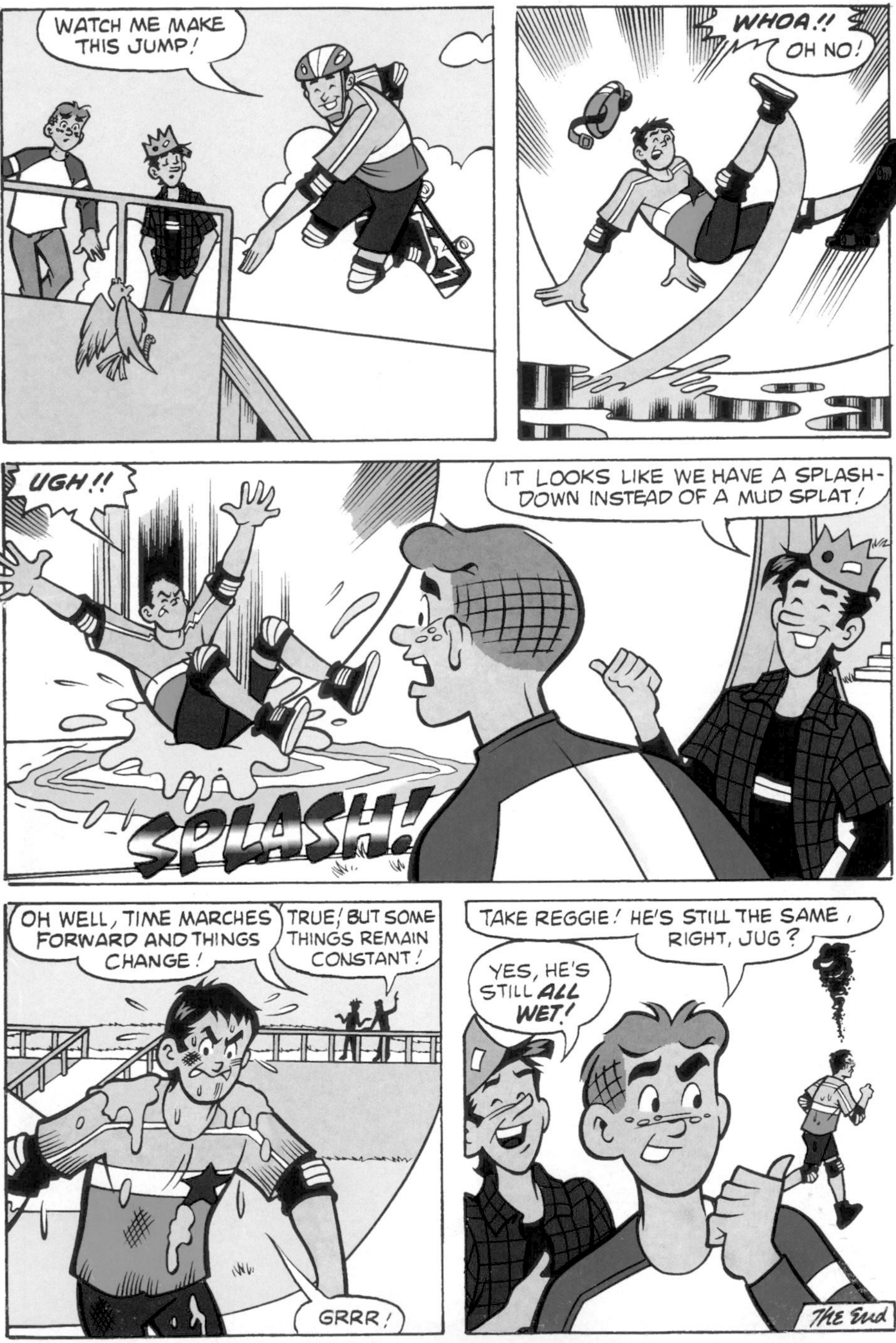
WATCH ME MAKE THIS JUMP!
WHOA!! OH NO!
UGH!!
SPLASH!
IT LOOKS LIKE WE HAVE A SPLASH-DOWN INSTEAD OF A MUD SPLAT!
OH WELL, TIME MARCHES FORWARD AND THINGS CHANGE!
TRUE; BUT SOME THINGS REMAIN CONSTANT!
GRRR!
TAKE REGGIE! HE'S STILL THE SAME, RIGHT, JUG?
YES, HE'S STILL ALL WET!
THE END